In the Shadow
of Our House

In the Shadow
of Our House

Stories by
Scott Blackwood

SOUTHERN METHODIST
UNIVERSITY PRESS
Dallas

Copyright © 2001 by Scott Blackwood
First edition, 2001
All rights reserved

Requests for permission to reproduce material from this work should be sent to:
Rights and Permissions
Southern Methodist University Press
PO Box 750415
Dallas, Texas 75275-0415

Some of the stories in this collection appeared first in the following publications: "In the Shadow of Our House" in the *Boston Review* (October/November 1999); "Prodigal Fathers" in *Gulf Coast* 10:2 (Summer 1998); "Worry" in *Other Voices* 27 (Fall/Winter 1997); "Nostalgia" in *Other Voices* 25 (Fall/Winter 1996); and "Riverfest" in *Whetstone* 13 (1996).

Grateful acknowledgment is made for permission to quote from the following: "This Is Just to Say" by William Carlos Williams, *Collected Poems: 1909–1939*, Volume I, New Directions Publishing Corporation; and "Don't Explain," Arthur Herzog Jr./Billie Holiday, Universal Duchess Music Corporation.

Jacket photograph by Nic Nicosia, *Real Pictures #11*, compliments of Nic Nicosia and Dunn and Brown Contemporary

Jacket and text design by Tom Dawson

LIBRARY OF CONGRESS CATALOGING-IN-PUBLICATION DATA

Blackwood, Scott.
    In the shadow of our house : stories / by Scott Blackwood.—1st ed.
      p. cm.
    Contents: In the shadow of our house — Nostalgia — Riverfest — One of us is hidden away — Alias — New Years — Worry — Prodigal fathers — One flesh, one blood.
    ISBN 0-87074-464-X (alk. paper)
    1. Austin (Tex.)—Fiction. I. Title.

PS3602.L33 I5 2001
813'.6—dc21   2001031353

For Ellie

ACKNOWLEDGMENTS

Thanks to the following people who offered their time and patience: Dean Blackwood, Rosa Eberly, Tommi Ferguson, Tom Grimes, Chris Haven, Debra Monroe, Scott Stebler, and Miles Wilson. Thanks, also, to Julie Fleenor at *Whetstone*, the Southwest Texas State MFA program, the Texas Commission on the Arts, and the Austin Writer's League. I am especially grateful to Kathryn Lang, my editor at SMU, for her enthusiastic support throughout.

*Maybe the thing you see coming from
far away is not the real thing, the thing that
scares you, but its aftermath. And what you've
feared will happen has already taken place.*

RICHARD FORD
Independence Day

CONTENTS

In the Shadow of Our House

I.

IF YOU HAD LIVED LONG ON OUR STREET, AND DRUNK late at our parties, you would know that before retiring and moving to Texas, Odie Dodd had been a government physician in Georgetown, Guyana. Squawking through the hole in his throat where his larynx had been before the cancer, Odie would have told how Jim Jones had asked him to the People's Temple to vaccinate the children. How malaria, cholera, bacterial meningitis slept in the jungle underbrush. How his truck had overheated along the rutted jungle road and he'd arrived a half-day late. How he was the first to find the bodies, though. Families. Limbs intertwined. Mothers sprawled over children as if sheltering them from some imminent hardship. Scattered on the dirt around them, dixie cups that had held the grape punch and cyanide. And already, of course, the smell. The uninterrupted whine of insects. At a party, Odie's hand would flatten his silver comb-over, and he'd say he hadn't known where he was for a time. That he'd wandered outside the compound and crouched in the shade of the jungle, the insect whine growing louder. In his daze, he glanced up into the canopy and for a moment it seemed it would descend on him. His scalp prickled. He called out. The feeling, he would say, was as in a dream when you know a terrible thing is about to happen but you are helpless to prevent it. But of course the thing had already happened. And then, if Odie had sipped enough scotch, and his wife Ruth had not yet touched his elbow to leave, he would have pulled you aside and asked the question he always asked of us: why was he spared? Later it would occur to you, as it did to Dennis Lipsy, that Odie had not been spared. And sometimes, when you are at the edge of sleep, witnessing calamities befall your children or your own can't-find-the-brake veering into oncoming traffic, Odie's fleshy hole appears.

This past summer, when Odie's backyard mangoes ripened and fell, we watched the grackles tear at them and said *he is dying*. Dennis Lipsy's son Isaac remembered Odie plucking the fruits in the evening, the fleshy wedges Ruth would slice and chill for our Fourth of July parties.

We watched Ruth's rigid steps to the mailbox, the weekly arrival of the yard man, to rake and bag leaves, shovel away rotting mangoes. When Ruth's sisters came down from Ft. Worth, we supposed the doctors wanted to remove more of Odie's organs but hoped he would put a stop to it, afraid we would see in his clinging our own graceless last hours. Those of us who had seen Odie and Ruth on the front stoop or climbing into Odie's van for doctor visits felt the exhausted tension between them. Averted eyes. Slumped shoulders. The living grappling with the dying. So we argued with our sons and daughters over unfinished yard work and waited for Ruth to tell us the news. To our surprise, no calls came. No family caravan of cars appeared. A few of us called. Did they need anything? No, a nice hospice nurse came to see them twice a week. Would they let us cook them a meal or two? Nothing agreed with Odie was the trouble. The medication was hard on him. His body is shutting down, we said, almost approvingly. Then, in late November, we heard his records playing through our open windows at night, just as we had when we first moved here, before our street joined the highway access road. Now as before, above the ether-whisper of our TVs, we heard scraps of Gershwin, Ella Fitzgerald's "Love Is Here to Stay."

When Ruth called to say Odie was gone, Dennis Lipsy—in the same barely audible voice that he used in our living rooms to explain probated wills and community property— told her how sorry he was. Did she want him to make the funeral arrangements? A pause and a gathering of breath. "Lord, I don't mean dead," she said, laughing, then catching herself. "He's wandering about."

That evening, Dennis gathered us in Ruth's living room, most still in work clothes, a few women corralling children in the dusky front yard. Ruth, unable to hold her hands still, told us the medication must have taken Odie out of his head. Before, she had always coaxed him back inside. The police, she said, had taken a report but nothing could be done until morning. What ditch will he be in by then? she'd snapped at Dennis, who stood as he usually did, slouch-shouldered, hands in pockets, impassive. For what seemed like minutes, Dennis was silent and we blamed him, thinking, now you have no answers, like us. But then something animated Dennis's body and he took her hands in his and quieted them. Some of us remembered years before when a car had clipped Isaac's bike at the street corner, how Dennis ignored us when we'd said maybe a head injury, don't move him. How Dennis plucked his son from beside the bike, parting us like reeds as he moved toward the speck of his wife Winnie at the end of the street.

In the living room, Ruth looked at her shoes. Would we like something to nibble on? she asked, looking up. She hadn't baked in such a long time, since before the cancer came back. No, we said, sweating in the warmth of the house, some of us noticing behind our thoughts the close, medicinal smell of the room. Then, in the backyard, the macaws began to shriek. Ruth laughed. "Well, someone has an appetite," she said.

If you were one of our sons, you might have scaled Odie's fence at night to blow marijuana smoke at his macaws, told later about opening the birds' cages, watching them careen into the dark, and how the next morning their red yellow blue plumes burned in the bare branches of your own cottonwood, their squawks laying blame. Odie and your father clanging pots and pans beneath the tree to chase the birds home, Odie himself squawking, saying he knew the responsible parties, bugger them. He might then have smiled at you, his sun-mottled face crimping, and you'd imagine him marking your brow for one of the dimpled balls he drove beyond his backyard fence, into the woods where you and your friends sometimes took girls.

"Odie dotes on these birds," Ruth said to us on the back porch, as if apologizing. Inside the cage, the macaws stabbed listlessly at the fruit she had sliced. Odie had told us macaws were often drugged and smuggled from South America in spare gas tanks. Intelligent, rare creatures, he'd said, some living to be octogenarians, outlasting numerous owners, knowing cruelty and kindness in all forms. They live in the shadow of our house. What might they tell us?

This is what we imagined: Odie and Ruth had a fight over the chemotherapy, Odie saying he didn't see the point and Ruth doing what she always did when distressed, going to the fish market for prawns to sauté with a green mango curry, Odie's favorite. On the way home, Ruth would have sat hunched over the wheel of her Plymouth, thinking of her father, who, his brain seized by an aneurysm, had lived with them the last three years of his life. Like Odie, he had given away bits of himself. Slivers of his frontal lobe to surgery, fluid to relieve pressure. He'd been a pilot in the early stages of World War II flying cargo planes of supplies to Great Britain but had been too old to fight. In the mid-1940s he had put on a weekly comedy show on a low-powered local radio station in Ft. Worth. A running skit about two rubes from the Panhandle lost in the city, she had told us. *Is that you, Leonard?* was his signature line. She remembered also late in his life, after the aneurysm, odd fragments of jokes resurfacing: *I had at one time a large, very fine ape. Did you now, Doctor? Oh yes, a lovely animal. But he grew suddenly ill and, not wanting to lose sight of him altogether, I made his skin into a mat for the table.*

We have seen a series of photos in their den that Odie took of Ruth's father. Every Monday at noon for three years, he posed the old man in the same chair in the same corner of the room. The lifelong cock of the old man's head growing ever more pronounced. A sly parting of his lips. *Is that you, Leonard?* His right eyelid gradually drooping over a six-week period up to where the photos ended. Good night, we have thought, seeing the last 3 x 5 near the bookcase. What was Odie after? Ruth isn't sure, though she knows it has to do with Jonestown, the axis around which his life winds. So she helped Odie position and sometimes cajole her father. In one photo, her disembodied hand clasps her father's shoulder as if he would topple sideways from the frame. And driving home from the fish market, it is beneath this photo on the wall that Ruth sees Odie, in the recliner, awake, but dreaming. He and Ruth are standing in an open field at a Ft. Worth airplane stunt show where they met in 1952. Ruth is gazing at the planes overhead, one hand shielding her eyes. She's lovely. He studies the smooth bend of her neck, the slender clavicle bone at its base. He's seized by the desire to percuss her sternum, though he is early in his residency and does not yet know the proper technique. She pulls in her lower lip slightly. He puts his hands in his pockets to hide his erection. She sees him, walks over and takes his arm, speaks close to his ear because of the drone of the planes, so close he can feel her breath and smell rose talcum on her skin. She says she's pregnant, though he knows her brief pregnancy and this event—their first meeting—are years apart. Ruth lets go of Odie's arm, bends at the waist near a water fountain, and vomits. Then she is ponderously heavy and back-bowed, her breasts full. By the time she waddles to the bleachers, her water breaks, gushing over Odie's feet like a great tide, sweeping his slippers from him. He is down on all fours looking for the goddamn things when she shouts at him. Odie looks up to see her mouth form a perfect circle, just as a stunt plane falters in its loop and noses into the field.

Odie crawled from the recliner and left the house in his bare feet. Nothing, other than Odie, is missing or out of place.

If you lived a street over, and happened to take your trash to the curb that evening, you might have seen flashlights flaring off trees along the creek bed, where we poked through the brush, looking for Odie. Instead we found refuse swept here by the flooding six months before: A child's mangled bike, mateless shoes, a large painted sign that welcomed baseball fans. Then, further in, beneath a limestone overhang, a dark bundle of sleeping bag we at first took for a man. A few of us lifted its saggy weight with sticks. Flattened on the smooth limestone ledge, a collection of bras and panties. We laughed nervously, some imagining awkward encounters in woods like these, the frantic peeling away of clothes, another's pale, taut skin against our own.

We slept fitfully. The macaws startled Dennis Lipsy awake with cries like small children's. His wife Winnie dreamed her long-dead parents were approaching the coast inside a giant sea snail. *Neogastropoda*. A name she told her husband later she couldn't get out of her head.

An article appeared in the next morning's paper with a photo of Odie. Sunfreckled. Gaptoothed. *Missing.*

Dogs give them away. Our sons' feet scuffle beneath Winnie Lipsy's lit window, where, through the curtains, they'd seen a scrap of breast. Some nights, we call out from our porches, threaten them with beatings. But before we can catch and wring them like wet towels, they are off across lawns and between the pine bones of the new duplexes we have for ten years fought off. We hear them scrape over the fence beyond the lots where they once built tree forts with stolen lumber. They are headed for the river, its fractured rise of train trestle, where they drink beer and climb the creosote rafters above the dark water, mocking us with the miraculous rise of their bodies.

Tonkawa Indians once raised their children along our river, not far from Red Bud Island where Dennis Lipsy takes his son fishing. Periodic floods washed over the banks then, even as they do now, carrying sediment, uprooting trees, unearthing the remains of their dead. But the Tonkawa always moved back, even occupying the same limestone shelters where their flood-lost sons and daughters once played, as if they could not help themselves. This is why, when they ate their captured enemies, the Comanches, as they often did, pregnant women were given the largest portions. Courage and strength. That is what they hoped to swallow.

II.

IN THE COOL OF THE EVENING, ODIE AND JIM JONES WALK along our street. Odie is barefooted.

Words fail, Jones says.

That's it? Words fail?

I'd place my hands on their shoulders, look at them with great sympathy—that was the hard part, you understand— then I'd say it. It was sincere. I couldn't think of anything else. I was shooting blanks.

They left you.

Not many, Odie. You'd be surprised.

They were afraid.

They sought rapture.

I think about it, the jungle.

"It has a fascination, too, that goes to work upon him." That's Conrad.

You asked me to come. On that day.

Coincidence. I forgot you were coming. Where the hell are your shoes, anyway?

You waited.

Christalmighty. Details. It was a busy time.

The cicadas were singing.

An axis around which your life winds. That's what they say, Odie.

Who says that?

Everyone.

You were in the kitchen when I found you, eating a melon.

The moment of the soul's attentiveness. Like Christ in the garden. Waiting.

For what?

For what God had to say. For the gun barrel at the back of my skull.

You were spitting melon seeds onto the floor.

The end, when it comes, is a small thing, a stick in the river—but it parts the water, alters its course, all the same. Otherwise the goddamn thing flows on. Tick without tock is nothing.

It was said you were dying. That you mistook your dying for theirs.

Words fail, Odie.

Yes, they do.

III.

IN THE EARLY MORNING, IF YOU JOGGED ALONG THE greenbelt at the base of our hill, you would glimpse patches of river through the cypress and cottonwood, and when you neared its bend where the trees gave way, scullers would glide past, their ebb and flow cutting a thin ripple in the glassy water behind. Eventually they would circle Red Bud Island, where, along the shore, Isaac tires of rebaiting his hook with minnows and skips rocks instead, saying the river smells like a wet dog. Beside him, Dennis remembering another time before, when he'd pointed downriver to where a rock outcropping had once formed an eddy, telling Isaac how they dynamited it long ago, that dozens of people drowned there in the 1920s. I wouldn't have, Isaac told him. I would've held my breath. Isaac's eyes narrowed and he sucked air, staring at the distant space in the river.

Once, while they were fishing, a black man had called them over to see what was on his trotline. He pulled from the water a three-foot alligator gar, its head narrowed into a long snout. Otherworldly. Early Pleistocene, the black man said, a damn antique. The gar slapped its slender body against the tree and the black man gripped its snout and tail, firm. Held it out for Isaac. Go ahead, the black man had said. Touch him. Some history there. When Isaac touched the clamped-shut teeth, he smiled sheepishly up at the man, and something sunk in Dennis's stomach. The black man let Isaac pick out a lure from his tackle box to keep.

A few times, Dennis had seen Odie along Shoal Creek, poking at rocky crevices with a hand spade, looking for awls, arrowheads, and the like. But there were other artifacts that he was partial to as well: rusted Sucrets boxes, television tubes, chrome knobs, watches, license plates. He kept an ancient yellowed pair of dentures wrapped in foil at home.

Odie once had held the dentures up, making for them a mouth with his hand. Had a tongue in it and could sing once, he'd said to Dennis and laughed until tears rose in his eyes.

We know some things: when she was nineteen, Winnie had lived with her instructor, a marine biologist at Texas A&M Galveston. She said she loved his sense of humor, and, of course, the sex, both of which had faded when in the late seventies they had spent nearly a year on the Mexican Baja, where he researched large sea mollusks. Winnie, tanned, in a wide-brimmed hat and red bikini top, stares out from the pages of a scrapbook we've seen. She's smiling but turned sideways, a hand holding the crown of her hat, as though reluctant to pose. Doubtful. This will not last, the gesture seems to say, as if she'd just conjured an image of the biologist's collection of unshelled mollusks floating in jars of formaldehyde in their extra bedroom. Only a few days after this photo was taken, she would find out she was pregnant. And Winnie thinking the nausea was a reaction to shellfish. When she had decided to have the baby, the marine biologist tried to hide his disappointment by throwing himself into books on prenatal care and natural childbirth. But his mood swung wildly. Once she found him naked on the kitchen floor wrapped in ice water–soaked bath towels. It's an Icelandic cure, he'd told her. For what? Pregnancy? she'd asked. And when she told him about the adoption, he'd fingered an embryology book —relieved, she knew—and asked, are you sure? in a voice that believed itself. At the hospital, he held her hand while she asked for the epidural. She did not look at him. She thought of a conch shell, hard, impervious. Afterwards, she did not want to hold her daughter, but her body demanded it. Her bones ached is what she would tell Ruth later.

And now, nineteen years later, she confessed to Ruth she sometimes caught herself absurdly scanning crowds at college football games on TV, or looking up suddenly while cooking dinner, drawn to a female voice on the evening news. She had even subscribed to a college fashion magazine and begun cutting out planky models she imagined having subtle intelligence and a sense of style.

The marine biologist tried to kill himself. Dennis had told us this at a party once. Not long after Winnie had left him and moved in with Dennis, he began calling at all hours. We all need to talk, the biologist said. There were threats, mostly about what he would do to himself, Dennis had said. Winnie had spoken gently to him, asked about his medication. Dennis had imagined him pickled in one of his jars. Then one day he came by Dennis's law office, and by chance Dennis wasn't at his desk. Instead, he and the biologist had stood one urinal apart in the office men's room, Dennis recognizing him from pictures he'd seen. But the biologist, knowing nothing more than Dennis's name, had stared at the shiny tiles, oblivious, a frayed look to his bearded face. He seemed someplace else. For a while afterward, Dennis felt weirdly exhilarated. But the biologist's expression had stayed with him. Dennis wondered if the biologist might be coming to an important decision about himself, something irrevocable. And when Dennis and Winnie were in Chicago a month later, Dennis kept thinking the biologist would pop out of a doorway or alley, although he knew he was thousands of miles away. And when they got lost coming back from Greek Town late one night, and crossed a metal drawbridge that spanned one of the channels feeding Lake Michigan, it occurred to him that he had not seen anyone else walking. That he'd gotten them lost. A few cars slipped by quickly, their tires ringing on the metal of the bridge. Below, he heard water lapping at the concrete sides of the canal. Winnie was tugging his shoulder, saying you lost bastard, in the giggly half-serious way she does right before she gets quiet and pissed. Then behind them, a voice said they were some lucky motherfuckers because Saturday night was lotto night, otherwise he wouldn't be out. Dennis had glanced back quickly, seized by the image of the biologist's stricken face. A bearded black man stared back. What y'all doing here? Should be home letting this man get into your sweetbreads. Dennis told Winnie not to turn around, only to keep walking. Winnie beside him, stiff, her eyes glancing down a cross street, thinking a cab, maybe a cab. And then a few seconds later, a cab did pass swiftly by, and inside Dennis could see moonlike faces lit up for a moment by oncoming traffic, then nothing. His stomach tumbled. Now two sets of footsteps behind. They walked on, faster. Someone kicked his heels and he stumbled slightly. Whoo, I smell something, a second voice said behind and laughed. Then a hand slapped

Dennis's ear. Ringing. He felt the ear with his fingers, looked at Winnie, wild-eyed, her face drawn. He wanted to tell her not to worry. Stay the fuck back, Nathan, the first voice said, these people with me. Feet scuffled. Dennis said he turned to see the two black men pressed against one another. And it struck Dennis suddenly that he and Winnie would be shot. They would bleed to death here simply because he had taken a wrong turn. He turned back, kept walking. Beside him, he heard Winnie say his name.

At the party, this is where Dennis paused, and then said it was a close call, that the second man had slunk off and the bearded man had taken them a quarter-mile to the elevated train and then, in front of the turnstiles, asked them for a twenty for the lotto. If I win, we'll split it, he'd said.

We imagined something else: Dennis and Winnie at the curb. The men behind. A few blocks away, a blue sign that said Dixie Cream Donuts. A light on inside where the baker was working. Three hundred yards. Run. The thought out before Dennis can stifle it. But we know this is our own weakness we are seeing and it settles like a stone in the belly.

Anyway, Dennis said at the party, when he and Winnie got back to the hotel, there was a message from a mutual friend that the biologist had shot himself.

Then the eggs, hundreds of them, arced through the dimming sky, and Odie stood transfixed. Outstretched hands cradled some eggs, fumbled others. Shrieks of laughter. Broken shells scattered on the grass. A few of us moved through the festival crowd toward Odie, children in face paint bumping our thighs. But when we got there, Odie was gone.

On the stage, a salsa band played, conga drums racing feverishly, then slowing. Trumpets blaring. Dennis thinking he'd seen Odie near the Maypole, barefoot, pants legs rolled, calmly eating a turkey leg. But when the song finished, he found himself staring at a Hispanic man in running shorts.

When darkness fell, the fire jugglers lit their batons and the crowd clapped wildly. The congas started up again. We milled about in the flickering shadows. The park police barking through a bullhorn that the park was closing, to grab your things. The crowd shouted back drunkenly, but gradually moved in ragged unison toward the park entrance. The congas kept on, gained momentum, indifferent to what was at hand. And just before the power was shut off and the world leaped into murmuring darkness, we saw Odie once more, being swept toward the entrance, his silver-haired head bobbing in the crowd, eyes fixed on the jungle canopy overhead.

Nostalgia

"YOUR NEW EYE LOOKS GOOD," MY WIFE NONA TELLS ME, sitting beside me on the front steps of the house we once shared. She puts her hand under my chin, turns my head towards her and stares into my prosthetic eye.

"Can you tell?" I ask.

She squeezes my arm gently, a distant familiarity reserved for soon-to-be ex-husbands. "Well, I knew you before," she says.

For half a minute, I say nothing, watch the sprinkler stream move over the yellow FOR SALE sign, onto flower beds and then back again. "Sometimes things I should've done differently stand out in relief," I say, surprising myself. I grin stupidly to cover my inexplicable seriousness, wondering how this comment will mesh with asking for my old lathe and table saw back.

"Please don't start," Nona says. "I'm happy with the way things are. I wish you were." Nona used to say, because I couldn't see the whole picture, I made up the other half.

But back then, beneath the joke, she had sympathy, even grudging love, for my attachment to the untapped possibilities of the past.

When we stood on these same steps eleven years ago, Nona's hands clutched her round belly, longing for this clapboard house with its Dutch gables, wraparound porch, the front yard, its oak branches lacing the blue sky. The realtor had given us a key to look around, telling us he'd be late. Inside, Nona opened all the bedroom windows, and we lay on our backs on the musty carpet, mentally furnishing sunflecked rooms. Nona rolled her round melon weight over onto me, her face flushed, her hands unbuttoning my jeans. I kissed her hard, hiked up her dress to the apex of her tight belly with its navel stem. The heavy, lurching rhythm of her moving against me, half-closed eyes.

Now, here on the porch, I'm overcome and want to kiss the nape of Nona's neck where a few wispy gray strands stand out against tanned skin. But this is out of the question. She looks hard at me and, for a moment, I wonder if she notices my eye's limited motion.

I look over at the large U-Haul backed into the driveway. "An Adventure In Moving," its black lettering says. Wes, Nona's intended, lopes down the ramp with an armload of orange blankets. Wes winks at us, his craggy face full of encouragement. He's been through these heart-to-hearts before, the wink says. But by late afternoon, he'll gleefully move Nona and my daughter Melissa down to San Antonio.

"I'm worried about you," Nona says, giving me a look that's sympathetic but not exclusively so. She's wondering if

I'll cause more trouble. That's a reasonable worry, I decide, watching boxes of albums, some of which are mine, leave in Wes's thick hands.

Last summer, I was arrested and put in jail for breaking into O. Henry's house. This was after Wes remodeled our kitchen and I found the Bill Monroe cassette he'd made for Nona. On the cassette, Wes's careful hand-lettering: "For Nona—High Lonesome Sounds." Nona even suggested having Wes over for dinner back then, a thank you for our expanded kitchen, she said. Besides, he and I had things in common. For instance: woodworking, bluegrass music, and, though she never said it, her. A part of me knew then where things were headed. I lost my appetite, dropped eight pounds. When something's missing, your body knows it before your head does.

Absent but not forgotten. That's what the embroidered plaque said hanging above O. Henry's wife's china cabinet. In the plaque's center, a washed-out photo of his wife, Athol, her hair pulled into a hard bun. I'd thrown a brick through the front window of the museum, crawled inside and later fell asleep on their quilted bed. "What were you thinking, Stan?" Nona said the next morning on the jail phone. I explained I'd gone drinking at Deep Eddy with a friend (which was true), and then blacked out (which wasn't). Sometimes what you're thinking can't be dovetailed with what you do, though Nona doesn't believe this. What was I thinking outside O. Henry's house? When I was a kid I read an O. Henry story about a dying woman who's saved by a fake leaf painted on the wall outside her window. Silly, sure, but this is what my reeling mind clung to, standing in O. Henry's front yard, brick in hand.

"Stan," Nona says to me now on the porch, narrowing her eyes, pale ovals of skin crinkling around them, "do you think you'll get married again?"

After a few seconds I realize this question is a kind of referendum, and what she's really asking is not so much my opinion on future marriage as it is: can we slough off one skin and enter another? Because she doesn't wholly believe she can.

"I'm seeing somebody," I say, surprising myself, the stupid grin returning. "A woman named Charlotte. She lives in Bastrop."

"Charlotte of Bastrop," Nona says in a dramatic voice. She smiles, genuinely happy for me.

"She has two teenage kids, Ben and Jennifer, so we try to be discreet." I watch Nona sweep her gray-brown hair from her face, tuck it behind her ear, then fiddle with an earring loop. She's interested, maybe even a little jealous. Charlotte's my ocularist. She took the putty mold of my eye socket and made me the eye, its painted hazel iris and red-dyed hairs for veins.

Charlotte and I have restoration in common. I run a furniture refinishing shop where I mostly restore antiques. Armoires, dining room tables, credenzas. Ornate, early-twentieth-century pieces. One afternoon, Charlotte brought in a glass-top oak display case she wanted refinished—"to display her eyes," she said.

She'd stared at my own eye, which, at the time, looked

like a pale grape. When I was ten, my grandfather's table saw kicked back a wedge of pine into it. Kids used to stare. At the rec swimming pool, I'd say, "Wouldn't open my eyes underwater if I were you," point to my eye. "Too much chlorine." My grandfather and I were in the toolshed when it happened. He yelled to me for his tape measure over the table saw's whining. I grabbed it from the shelf, pulling the tape out long, and cut the air with it, a sword. The wedge of pine made a thwacking sound against my skull. Later, my grandfather joked to hide his awkwardness, saying, "Stan thrust when he should've parried." How different would things be if I had?

I looked the display case over. After I explained the sanding and staining process, she said, "Ruptured cornea?"

"What?" I said, like I hadn't heard.

"Your eye," Charlotte said.

"Something's wrong with it?" I said.

She smiled. "I could make you a new one—but it's just for looks." She paused. "Some people misunderstand."

"I'm on the transplant list," I said. I wanted to hop in my truck, head home, my ruptured eye still containing the possibility of sight, however slight. Staying meant closing off options.

She stood with one bare leg crossing the other, looking at me, an appraisal, while I gave a refinishing estimate. I was staring at the pad, but I could see a silver anklet circling the hard ball of her ankle.

"I make beautiful eyes," she said. I looked up quickly, my heart thudding.

On the porch with Nona, I crunch ice between my teeth and look down at the Pattersons' adjoining lawn, where a kiddie pool sits and two bikes sprawl on their sides. Across the street a mower starts up. My shirtless, tanned former neighbor Earl Gunter appears along the side of his house, an allergen mask strapped over his nose and mouth, dust and dry grass swirling around him. He sees us and waves cautiously, as if saying, I've done all I can for you both, so keep your future plans to yourselves. Earl's in his sixties. A retired justice of the peace. He has good reason to think I'm a nut—he went with Nona to bail me out of jail—though he never lets on that he does. It says something about me that I avoid him now. I give him a hearty wave from behind the windshield of my truck every time I pick up Melissa for a visit.

It's getting hot on the porch, concrete warming the backs of my thighs. Wes ambles up, still grinning, asks if I could help him with a few boxes. "Sure thing," I say, and for a second I feel the urge to shove him down the steps. Then it passes. I walk inside my former house and a hollowness settles in my stomach. My shoes squeak on the living room's parquet flooring. Wood I cut, laid and stained.

People used to grow old and breathe their last raspy breaths under their own roof. I remember my grandfather's house, the skin-tightening warmth of space heaters, the smell of Mentholatum. His bed faced the window, where, outside, bloated tomatoes hung on a trellis. His cataract eyes couldn't see the vines, though we pretended they could. Sons and daughters hovering. Help me roll him over, someone said. Rust-colored bedsores. The outline of his body in the mattress, a mold, where he'd been. Later, though I wasn't in the room, his teeth ground, his white-crusted lips parted. He's gone, someone said. A county nurse's slender hand gripped the oak bedpost. In the window light, dust motes (his sloughed-off skin and ours) carrying souls (my grandma said this) from our earthly house to the other, beyond.

This is what I want to know: How much dust has already floated away and how much is me now?

Through the front window, I can see Nona looking over her plants, deciding which ones to take. Across the street, my ex-neighbor Earl is sitting on his porch, wiping his face with a towel. Bags of grass neatly line the road in front of his house. Look at that poor son of a bitch, he's probably thinking, as I pack my wife and kid off to another man's house.

"You okay there, Stan?" Wes says in front of me as he heads down the steps with a cardboard box.

I'm sweating now, a belated hangover from last night. What will happen if I pass out, go crashing down with Nona's china? "I'm fine," I say, and remember how last December, a few months after the separation, I got high late one night and decided to come over and put up Christmas lights for Nona when she was on her shift at the hospital. A favor, I thought in my daze. I still had a key. So I pulled the boxes of Christmas decorations from the attic, grabbed a ladder from the toolshed, and climbed onto the roof. It was cold and I blew on my hands while pulling strings of lights across the roof. I stepped on a loose shingle and slid. Down went the lights pow pow pow onto the driveway, like firecrackers. I tried to get back up but I'd twisted my ankle. I thought about yelling for help, then I thought about the state I was in. Half-gone. Semi-departed. From where I sat, I could see Earl and his wife Clara standing in their kitchen window, watching. In my addled, never-still mind, I imagined Earl dialing Nona at work, saying I was crazy.

I crawled back up against the chimney and held my ballooning ankle and watched my breath billow, then disappear.

Riverfest

"HOW ABOUT A KISS?" PHIL SAID, LEANING INTO THE yellow-lit ticket window where his wife Helen was counting twenties.

"Oh, here we go. You are so needy," Helen said. She leaned over the counter, kissed him. She readjusted the pin on her shirt pocket that said RIVERFEST, a catfish in a Stetson grinning beneath the lettering.

Phil looked off at their daughter Katy climbing into the Moonwalk, her sock feet denting rubber mounds. "A little affection can't hurt." He dug one of his keys into the lino- leum counter and then tried to smudge the gouge away with his thumb. "It's a *trial* separation. Nothing's set in stone."

She bit her lip and looked around Phil at the line be- ginning to form. "It's just that you always think to do things when they're least helpful."

"You said you'd get off early tonight."

"I said I'd *try*. You're embarrassing me."

"You open, lady? You selling tickets?" boomed a male voice at the back of the line.

Phil turned. A freckle-faced man glared at him. "She's my wife," Phil said. "No problem. She'll sell you some tickets, just hold your horses." He grabbed a loop of tickets from Helen, walked to the next booth and bought a beer. He sat down on a bench adjacent to the ticket booth. He looked at his wife under the light, the blond fuzz along the edge of her cheekbone. She flirted with a college kid and his friends, her eyes widening.

Three months ago his life had seemed tangible and mapped. He'd gotten a small promotion at Southwestern Bell Telephone, and they'd started paying back money Helen's dad loaned them on the house. Katy started kindergarten in a year, and they could save the money they'd been spending on her preschool. They saw the rough outline of where they wanted to be, like the V in the river current you pointed a canoe toward. Then everything turned hazy. Helen quit Foley's after a supervisor accused her of taking a pair of gold earrings.

When Phil picked her up at the mall entrance, her eyes were puffy and red. "I should've really stolen something from that bastard," she'd said. "I'd feel better."

Afterwards, they bought a bottle of wine at the Tom Thumb and he drove his telephone truck down a dirt road along the river. The truck shuddered over ruts and the glove box fell open. Behind them, Phil could see dust rising. He called in on his radio and told the office the radiator had overheated.

His throat felt tight.

"You're pissed, aren't you." She slipped her heels off.

"No. I'm not pissed. It's frustrating is all," he said. "You can't collect unemployment when you quit."

"God. I can tell you're pissed. You're not even looking at me." Her voice wobbled. She sipped wine from a coffee cup.

"He's a prick. It wasn't your fault. I know that." He looked at her, then back at the road.

"I should file a complaint, sue him," she said, arching her ass off the seat, tugging at pantyhose.

Phil took the coffee cup from her and swallowed what was left. Along the rim were pink crescents of lipstick. The radio squawked, and he turned it off.

Helen held his hand in her lap with her eyes closed. She rubbed his arm.

His head throbbed behind the fuzziness of the wine. Ahead, the dirt road and sky merged into a dirty vanilla. Between the cypress, he saw scraps of the river.

Helen pulled his hand under her skirt and moved against it. He felt his cock stiffening, pushing against his jeans. After a little while, she stopped, moved his hand aside. She put on his Southwestern Bell hard hat, pulling it low over her eyes, and sat cross-legged on the seat.

"Sometimes it's like I'm watching this other person and I'm not me at all," she said.

On the way to pick up Katy at school, he'd surprised himself. They drove through the mall parking lot and stopped along a row of cars in front of Foley's. Sunlight glared off the windshields. "Which one's his?" he said, arms folded over the steering wheel. He used the corkscrew on his Swiss Army knife to puncture the bastard's tires. Helen sank down in the seat, eyes wide, her hand covering her mouth. He imagined how he must look: a stranger slinking between cars, brushing gravel from his knees as he climbed into the truck. For a minute, he wondered if their marriage had infected him, made him like her—as if he stood outside himself, watching.

Helen screened calls with the answering machine for weeks, afraid that someone had seen them. She slept late, and Phil made Katy's lunch, dressed her, took her to preschool. Usually by the time they left, Helen would be sitting at the kitchen table with a highlighter pen, drinking coffee, flipping through the classifieds. One afternoon, a woman's voice on the answering machine asked if Helen had forgotten their interview.

Bills went unpaid. Once, they'd argued over a six-dollar jar of artichoke hearts Helen bought. He'd followed her into the bathroom, grabbing her arm, saying she was going to have to eat every goddamned one of those hearts.

At the Riverfest, Katy waved from inside the Moonwalk and Phil waved back. A siren wailed at a game booth where kids shot water into clowns' mouths. *We have a winner on lucky number three,* a carnie shouted. Two booths down, a woman's voice yelled: *Is love on your horizon? Will you come into money? Have children? Marlina the Oracle reads palms, reveals the future before your eyes.*

A month ago, on Helen's birthday, they ate at Mexico Tipico and talked about separating. She picked at a beer label, balling wet paper between her fingers. "We hardly do anything together except fight," she said. "We're good parents though, aren't we? I'm proud of that." They held hands across the table, ate flautas and guacamole and discussed how they'd divide the weeks with Katy. Helen talked about the hours she'd picked up at the Riverfest, how it would be steady through summer. Maybe she'd make a job contact.

She ordered two more beers and grabbed a napkin and a pen, and they decided on what furniture he would need and where he might live. They needed a timetable. "How about the end of the month?" Helen said, calm as if they were planning a camping trip. They would have to sell some things to pay his first month's rent. As it was, they were behind on the car payments. When she went to the bathroom, he looked at the list on the napkin and felt his stomach flop.

That night, he waited until Katy was asleep and slept on the hide-a-bed. In the dark living room his movements seemed loud and unsure, and he lay motionless. He wondered if he and Helen would sleep together occasionally. He thought of other women he knew and he imagined what their bodies might feel like. For a short time he felt relieved, even expectant, but an apprehensiveness came over him when he started looking at apartments, walking through dank-smelling rooms where couches and beds had left quarter-size depressions in the carpet. He thought of the seven years it had taken them to become familiar with each other, a family. At night he looked through photo albums, pictures of Katy in the maternity ward, the white explosion of the flash on the window.

At the festival, the carnie's voice blared: *Not a hoax, not a fake, Marlina's the real thing.* A giant red neon sombrero wheeled and tilted near the Ferris wheel. The air smelled like funnel cakes and sausage. Lightning flashed across the river. The wind picked up, and strings of colored lights over the midway swayed. Phil bought another beer and watched Katy in the Moonwalk. She jumped from one inflated mound to another and then tumbled. Phil wondered if his life had always been capricious and he'd somehow blinded himself. He was in a movie in which the scenes were out of sequence. If only he could step out, he could link the beginning, middle, and end. Condensation was building up on the Moonwalk's plastic windows and Katy's face blurred as if he were remembering her. After the sky grew dark, Phil asked the baggy-eyed Moonwalk attendant to tell Katy it was time to go. She wobbled into the doorway, cheeks flushed. She scowled. "You said we'd stay late."

"It's starting to rain, goose. We'll come back."

Carnies scurried around booths, unfolding tarps. Phil held Katy's hand and they moved toward the parking lot. Helen waved at them as they passed; Katy tugged loose from his hand, blew kisses. When they reached the car, Phil buckled Katy in the seat and looked back at the ticket booths, their shutters drawn, slivers of yellow light beneath. They pulled away as rain plunked against the roof and windshield.

At home, Phil put Katy in the bathtub and started packing boxes. In three days, he'd move. He was sorting through photos when the phone rang. He picked it up.

A woman's voice said, "Is this Phil Peoples?"

"Yes, who's this?"

"Daddy, close the curtain for my magic trick," Katy said.

The woman cleared her throat. In the background Phil heard a TV laugh track. She hung up.

"Is that Momma?"

"No, sweetie, just someone with the wrong number." How did the woman know his name? He imagined her pulling it out of the phone book at random. A stranger's finger moving down the column, settling on Peoples.

Katy said, "I'm full of magic. Magic toes." She kicked at the water, splashing some onto the floor.

"Water stays inside, Magic Katy," Phil said, squatting beside the tub. He squeezed a glob of shampoo onto her hair and rubbed it in. "How do you feel about me living someplace else?"

Katy pinched her eyes shut and didn't say anything.

"Nothing will change when I leave. It's just that you'll have two homes. It'll seem hard at first, like when you started school, but then it'll seem normal." He stared at his foaming hands and realized he was waiting for Katy to say she understood, to conspire with him against the oncoming changes. He saw her indistinct face in the Moonwalk window and a tiredness crept into his body.

"If you want to see my magic trick, close the curtain," Katy said, molding her sudsy hair into a spike. "Momma will appear before your eyes."

On Saturday morning, rain fouled up their yard sale, and they pulled everything into the garage. Katy sprawled on a sleeping bag near the washer. Suits and dresses hung from wires strung between ladders. Alongside Phil's maroon Camry squatted appliances, toys, a stereo, the gold-colored hide-a-bed. Helen sat drinking coffee and looking at *House Beautiful,* her bare leg propped on a card table, her skirt open, revealing pale inner thighs, green panties. "How's your head?" Phil asked.

"Thumping," she said, not looking up. "I'm not going to be much help."

"So where'd you go, party girl?" Phil said, popping her on a thigh with a newspaper.

She glared.

"Come on. That didn't hurt."

"Goddamn, I hate it when you do that," she said. "Like you're my big brother."

"I was teasing," Phil said. His face felt hot. "It was just a tap." He turned to Katy. "I was teasing."

"I want someone to watch this with me," Katy said from the sleeping bag. "I don't like when Fievel Mousekewitz falls off the ship."

Phil said, "In a minute, sweetie. Mommy and Daddy are talking."

Helen's arms hugged her chest and she walked to the front of the garage.

"So, what did you do?" he said, following her.

"After the festival some of us went out."

"Seems reasonable." Phil felt a thin smile forming on his lips. He wanted to hit her, to see his trembling fingers clap to her mouth, her teeth blood-flecked.

"What's gotten into you?" Helen asked, looking at his face, then at his hands.

"You," he said, wedging his hands into his jeans pockets.

By afternoon, water stood in low places in the yard. The acoustic ceiling above Phil's Camry had darkened and then started to leak. A tropical storm was moving through, the radio said.

They had sold some CDs, a few of Katy's toys and a blender. When the rain let up, Helen put Katy down for her nap and left for the festival.

Phil sat at the card table in the garage going through a stack of mail: a letter from Visa saying they were canceling his account, another from the bank saying he was behind on his payments, and they would regret turning his car loan over to collections. He opened a brochure about a cruise in the Bahamas, a picture of a man and woman snorkeling in a clear blue lagoon. *Pack your bags* it said. He tossed the brochure in a pile.

A stooped man in a rain poncho picked through Phil's ties. He spread each one across his palm, examined it. Phil picked up a box of CDs and began separating them into two stacks. He thought about taking a second job. His cousin Teddy sold water filter systems on the side, opening a large plastic suitcase on coffee tables. Tubes, canisters, charcoal filters. "We're mostly water," he once told Phil. "Why not make sure it's pure?"

The phone rang inside the house.

"Phil Peoples?" a woman's voice said when he answered it.

"Yes."

"My name's Melanie Wiede."

Silence.

"Did you call me last night and hang up?" he said.

"I did. I'm sorry. I lost my nerve." She cleared her throat. "I was just shaken so bad, I was afraid I wouldn't do this right."

"Who are you?"

"I'm calling about your wife. She's having a relationship with my husband."

Something in Phil's stomach tightened. He looked out the front window at a brown Volvo slowing down, a bald man inside gesturing at a woman beside him.

"Mr. Peoples?" the woman said softly.

"Yes." He leaned his back to the wall away from the window and took deep breaths.

"This is crazy, isn't it? I always thought I'd know. I'd just be able to tell by the way he acted, by the way he smelled or some stupid thing like that."

"I think this is a mistake," he said.

"I hired a detective to watch him. That's terrible, isn't it?"

"No," he heard himself say. "It would be all right if you had reasons." His face felt greasy. He took his glasses off and wiped them with his shirt front. With one hand, he felt the stubble along his chin. He pictured Melanie Wiede, dark half-circles under her eyes, calling from a pay phone, her body wedged into a corner, fingers twisting her hair.

"I've got two little boys," Melanie said. In the background, a car honked.

"This detective. What did he find out?"

"Well, that they're fucking," she said softly.

"I understand that," Phil said. "What kind of proof are we talking about?"

"I know you're having a tough time. Maybe this isn't a good idea."

"I'm glad you called." He heard his voice crack. "I don't know what to do." His hand on the phone felt cold. Blood had stopped circulating.

"You sound like a sweet man. You have a daughter, right?"

"How did you know that?"

"The detective. He says what sometimes happens is that the one doing the fooling around sues for custody as a preemptive measure."

He rubbed his temples. "How long has it been going on?"

"Three months," Melanie said. "I've got some pictures." Silence.

"Phil, I'm sorry. I thought we could help each other."

It was dark when Phil started with Helen's dresser. He tossed her panties and bras on the bed. Nothing. Then the sock drawer. A small brown sack lay in one corner, stuffed with old cards, photos. He opened each card, and in most he found his own handwriting from years before. His words struck him now as ridiculous. *I'm closer to you than I've been to anyone.* School pictures of Katy, the coached ladylike crossing of legs, the faint trace of a scar on her chin where she'd fallen on the front steps. The sweater drawer. He pulled condoms from a box and counted them. He thought of Helen's freckled shoulders. The image of her pale thighs straddling a faceless Wiede in a swivel chair came to him. He sat on the bed and dumped out the rest of the drawers, scattering sweatpants, T-shirts. In a lacquered wood jewelry box in the bottom drawer he found eight pairs of gold earrings still in their gray velvet boxes.

He untucked the bedsheet, held the corners up and folded all of Helen's things into it like a seine. He waited at the front door until the timed streetlight dimmed, then carried his load outside. The street was wet and the air stuck to his skin. He grabbed the tire iron and a flashlight from the trunk of the Camry. Near the curb, he pried up the storm drain cover. Grinding, then clanging against concrete. Staring into the hole. The rushing of water. Tumbling Helen's things in. He looked over at the neighbors' house. Jim Bowden at the kitchen window, a slice of pizza drooping in his hand.

When Katy woke up from her nap, it was nearly 7:30. Phil warmed her a hot dog in the microwave, and they left for the festival. On the way, he stopped at a gas station, got out. Across the river, the sky was orange from the festival lights, and he could hear music.

After he'd pumped the gas the intercom voice said, "We've got a problem."

"What's that?" Phil said, tightening the gas cap. He watched Katy in the back seat, playing with dolls.

"You need to come back inside, fella. Your credit card's no good."

"I've got some cash at the house. It's just a few blocks away." He waved at Katy, who was giving him a strange, round-eyed look.

"No, sir. I've already had five drive-offs. It's my ass if I let you go."

Phil looked over at the window where the attendant was standing. The man's silver hair was combed back from his forehead, and he wore a dark blue smock that said Phillips 66. "It's been a bad day," Phil said. "Try the card again."

The attendant threw up his hands. "I've tried it. I need cash, credit, something. Goddamn, son. Call somebody and have them bring you the money."

Phil felt something hard rise up in his chest. "You can have my watch," he said, starting to pull it off his wrist. "I'll come back."

"I can't take your watch. Call somebody or I'll have to call the cops."

"I've got a kid out here," Phil's voice echoed back from the building. He looked through the window at the bright packages of chips and candy, the Marlboro Man smoking a cigarette near the attendant's booth. Then he moved around the front of the car. Katy lay curled like a shrimp on the back seat.

The attendant met him on the driver's side, his hand on the door. "Now fella, you don't want to get in that car," he said. "You'll get us in all sorts of shit."

Phil shouldered the attendant out of the way and tugged at the door handle. As he pulled it open the attendant grabbed him around the waist, pinning his arms. Small plastic men and women tumbled from the car. "Watch out now," the attendant's voice wheezed behind Phil's head. Then the scraping of shoes on concrete, being pulled backwards. Phil's arms swinging, hitting shoulder blade, muscle, then something soft that made a popping sound and the attendant lay on the ground, not moving.

Phil got in the car. Katy crawled over the seat, gripped his arm with both hands, crying. She had peed a dark circle on the gray upholstery. They'd have to go home to change. "The man's okay, sweetheart. He's going to get some ice for his bruise, like at school," Phil told Katy. His breath came in heaves and his stomach felt hollow. He looked in the rearview mirror at the attendant, who was still sitting on the oil-stained cement, holding his head. "He wanted to steal our car," Phil said, feeling ashamed as soon as he'd said it. Katy's teeth chattered.

Phil started the car and pulled onto the road. He felt capable of anything now, a stranger to himself, like Helen. He remembered the Foley's Christmas party, Helen across the living room, holding a glass of wine, talking to a tall man he didn't recognize. She wore a black dress; her shoes were off and she poked the carpet with her toes. He remembered feeling there was an intimacy to her body, to her feet, that he couldn't share. He'd looked away. In the clamor of opening gifts, Helen came into the kitchen. "I looked for you," she said, kissing him. "Where'd you go?"

• • •

At the festival, Katy clung to Phil's hand. The grounds were muddy and pitted with sour-smelling puddles. A child's tennis shoe stuck out of the mud near the porta-toilets. It started to sprinkle, so they found a vendor's tent, and he dug into his pockets for change to buy a lemonade. A fat vendor woman handed Katy her lemonade and smiled at her, asking if she'd ridden the Tilt-A-Whirl yet. Katy shook her head, then pressed her face against Phil's leg.

Phil remembered yesterday's loop of tickets in his pocket. "You want to go on some rides? Does that sound fun?" he said, forcing a smile.

"I want to see Momma." Katy's eyes followed a man in a catfish suit handing out balloons by the ticket booths.

"We will, baby, but we've got all these tickets. Let's take the Ferris wheel." How had the night gotten so out of hand? He suddenly wanted to call Melanie Wiede, hear her voice. He looked around for a pay phone. Behind them, telephone lines stretched from roofs of carnie trailers, disappearing up utility poles. He wasn't sure he had a quarter.

"It won't be scary, right?" Katy said.

Phil sipped lemonade, his hand shaking.

Below them, the festival was a mass of swirling light. Marlina the Oracle's giant crystal ball gleamed from the top of her trailer, a large mechanical eye blinking. Shiny Tilt-A-Whirl shells spun.

In the distance, Phil could see the river swelling, its chalky banks disappearing, motionless black water cresting as in an overfilled bathtub.

Katy pointed. "They're so tiny. People look like bugs."

People were lined up in front of the swirling sombrero. Two security men with walkie-talkies on their belts talked with a group of teenage girls.

"Daddy, that boy was spitting," Katy said, wrinkling her nose.

Phil narrowed his eyes. Near the music pavilion, he saw Helen dancing with a bearded man, her hand at the small of his back. She wore a white sleeveless shirt, her hair pulled back in a ponytail. Then the steel guitar stopped whining and the crowd clapped. Phil twisted in the seat for a better look, his hips wedged hard against the safety bar as the Ferris wheel lurched down. They swung past a carnie with long sideburns, talking to a girl. Then they rose again. The carnie uncrossed his arms, seeing Phil half out of the chair. "Hey!" he shouted, waving.

The wind had picked up, and the seats rocked back and forth. Katy squeezed his hand. He thought about going home, putting Katy to bed. He'd wait for Helen, ask her how long she'd known the bearded man. Then he remembered when they were first married, Helen insisting that they never go to sleep angry at one another.

His hands were cold. Beads of water collected on his glasses, and when he wiped them on his shirt, he thought two things: it had started to rain, and he now understood why men kill their wives.

• • •

It was late when Phil pulled into the driveway. Helen's car was still gone. Katy had fallen asleep on the way home from the festival and Phil carried her inside, put her on the couch. He sat down, switched on the TV, flipped through channels, then turned it off and sat in the dark. He heard the refrigerator humming in the kitchen, Katy's steady breathing.

The doorbell rang.

Phil opened his front door and found Jim Bowden standing on the porch, looking down at a planter full of basil gone to seed. "I wasn't quite sure what to do with this," Jim Bowden said, taking a wadded black bra from his windbreaker and handing it to Phil. He smiled, then sucked his lower lip. "Found it in the yard before the police got here." He sniffed. "I asked what the problem was, but they wouldn't tell me. They asked if I'd seen you. I said, no, I hadn't." He ran his fingers over his mustache. "I didn't tell them anything. I said you were working late." Bowden looked past Phil at Katy, open-mouthed, sleeping on the couch. "So. Anyway." Jim Bowden paused, still standing in the doorway, patting a hand against his thigh. "Just wondered if you needed some help." The phone rang and Phil went into the den and answered it. "Phil?" a woman's voice said. "It's Melanie. Can you talk?"

Phil didn't say anything. He waved at Bowden from the den. Bowden nodded. "Sure. Yes," Phil said into the phone, his heart quickening.

Jim Bowden said, "Wanted you to know that Anita and I are here for you guys," his voice trailing off.

"God, are you all right?" Melanie asked.

"No. I'm really not." Phil's body slackened. He imagined Helen straddling Wiede, her quick breath. Himself stretching a phone cord between his fists. Helen, wide-eyed, rising. He shoves her back. The cord pinching the skin of her neck. Her face turning newborn blue.

"Can we meet somewhere? My mother has the kids," Melanie said.

"Let me know," Jim Bowden said in a low voice, waving his hand, moving out the door.

At six the next morning, Phil's supervisor called him in to repair lines knocked out during the storm. Two policemen had stopped by the office last night looking for him, his supervisor told him.

"Must be a mix-up," Phil said, opening a slat in the kitchen blinds with his fingers. Rain slanted onto the windowsill.

"You mind giving them a call?" his supervisor said.

"You bet." In the backyard, stepping stones were sunk beneath a muddy stream.

After he hung up with his supervisor, he tried to eat an English muffin but couldn't get it down. He wrote a note to Helen, who was asleep, saying she needed to watch Katy for the day. He stuck the note on the refrigerator and left.

After work, he drove to the Pier and Beam, which stood on pilings near the river. Tables—normally crowded with state employees and students from the university—were mostly empty. Candles flickered in glass globes. James Brown shouted from speakers.

Waiting for Melanie at the bar, Phil watched a girl with a curved nose sitting sideways on her boyfriend's lap. She was using a pair of nail clippers to carve their names into the table—a tradition at the bar. The back of her dress plunged halfway down her back to a constellation of moles. Her boyfriend whispered something in her ear. "You wish," she said, laughing, tilting her head.

He remembered years before—when he first started dating Helen—coming here after skiing the wide part of the river with his brother's boat. She wore an orange one-piece and her skin smelled like coconut and her milk-coffee hair hung to the middle of her back. Sipping his beer, he tried to remember if they'd carved their names. Through the window he could see car lights on the road below. He wondered if it was Melanie Wiede.

"All skin and no bone," someone said. Laughter. Smoke haloing light fixtures.

Fat drops of rain slapped against the deck. The wind blew through open windows, scattering coasters.

"You don't have a goddamn clue," the curved-nose girl said in a sleepy, drunken voice.

Billie Holiday sang from the speakers. *Hush now, don't explain, you're my joy and pain.*

Out on the deck a large tree branch clattered against the wood railing. Marble-sized hail thumped against the roof and deck. Phil thought of the Camry in the parking lot.

"Up your ass," the curved-nose girl said, and he realized

she was staring at him. "You've been looking over here." She pushed her nose up with her fingers like a pig's snout.

"I'm just having a drink," he said, looking from her to the boyfriend, whose face seemed haggard and distrustful in the candlelight.

A tall woman with dark, curly hair moved onto the stool beside him. She slid a manila envelope onto her lap. A red-striped umbrella pooled water on the bar. Her hands were tan and slender, the nails painted pink. She looked at the door then turned to him. "Hi, Phil. I'm Melanie," she said. "I recognized you from the detective's photos." She held out her hand and he shook it, his heart thudding in his chest.

He wondered if, in the photos, he looked like the kind of man who'd throw his wife's clothes down the storm drain.

They moved to a table beside a small stage cluttered with amplifiers and stacks of chairs. Along the wall hung fuzzy black-and-white photographs of a flooded river, crumbled limestone bridges, a grinning policeman pointing to a tractor tire in a cypress, a clapboard house being swept over a dam.

The boyfriend was holding the curved-nose girl by the arm, heading out the door.

Melanie scooted the manila envelope on the table and the metal latch made a scratching sound. "Phil, you should understand that I'm not doing this out of a pure heart. I'm really going to stick it to Andy. You should know you might have to be a witness."

"I guess I understand." He asked the waitress for two beers. The table was scarred with names and dates. Next to his car keys was an inscription: Ty and Barbara '79. He looked at the faint creases around Melanie's eyes, dark eyebrows. He leaned forward slightly. "I think I may have put a man in the hospital yesterday. I just lost it. At the gas station. I hit him right in front of my little girl."

"You sounded sad on the phone." Her voice was quiet. "These last days must have been awful. I can't see—"

"They turned down my credit card." He tried to think of what happened, tried to break down the gas station incident into frames, like a videotape.

"Did he threaten you?"

He wondered how long before it caught up with him, imagined Helen holding Katy at the kitchen table, policemen asking questions. "What?" he said. A saxophone blared.

"You wouldn't have hit a man unless he threatened you."

"I'm not sure what happened."

"I wish it would've been Andy you hit," she said evenly. The waitress put the beers on the table and Melanie slid hers back and forth. She pulled her hair back and Phil could see a spiraled silver earring dangling from her lobe, the smooth skin of her neck. "Do you think I'm crazy?" she asked.

"Christ, I'm beating people up." The lights flickered.

"So where did Helen meet your husband?" Phil said.

Melanie took a swallow of beer. "At Foley's. They'd take their lunches in my husband's office. That's a euphemism Mr. Kinnard, the detective, uses. *Take their lunches.* I laughed when he told me. I'm sure he thinks I'm crazy." She smiled and the creases around her eyes widened.

"You're not."

Melanie placed her hand over his. "Thank you," she said.

Phil imagined kissing her, the moist warmth of her mouth. His lips on her neck, breasts. Helen's blue face came back to him.

The bar was nearly empty. Outside, it had stopped raining. Branches and trash lay scattered on the deck. Melanie ordered bourbon. She got up to go to the bathroom, bent over, kissed him on the cheek, her breasts hovering near his shoulder.

He stood up, opened the doors, and stepped out onto the deck. The air was cool and still. Water ran from the gutters. A half-moon appeared. In the parking lot below, a great pool of water stretched like a dark island. He could see flecks of quartz in the gravel. Beyond the road, the river rushed through fingerlike cypress roots, over grass and saplings and stone. Dissolving muddy banks. Farther down the river the mud and silt would form a new bank. Loss and compensation everywhere. He felt weak, emptied.

Through the doors he could see the table, the manila envelope next to their beer bottles. He tried to conjure a distant future, a time when the trouble would settle, but all he could see were the burning lights of his house, Helen's and Katy's tight, exhausted faces.

He wondered why Melanie was gone so long, if she'd gotten sick. He would have to take care of her. He'd walk her up the front steps of her house, her head against his chest. "Where are we now?" she'd ask, blinking in the porch light. "I brought you home," he'd say.

He walked to the table and undid the latch on the manila envelope. In a 5 x 7 photograph, Katy helped him wash the Camry, suds rolling off the driveway. In another, the Camry was parked in front of his house. In the bay window, halved in shadow, he saw himself, talking on the phone. Where were the pictures of Helen and Wiede?

The lights flickered again and a jazz song started over. Phil went down a hallway to the bathrooms.

"Melanie, are you all right?" he called, knocking on the bathroom door, then opening it.

Silence.

He looked under the stalls. Empty.

He ran outside with the envelope under his arm, loping down the steps to the parking lot. From the top of a utility pole a transformer buzzed. A large cottonwood branch had broken off and fallen onto the wires. Its weight dipping the wires halfway to the ground, a sling. A crew would have to repair them.

The Camry was gone.

He fumbled in his pockets for his keys. She'd taken them.

Blue sparks leapt from the transformer. The air had a burnt smell. He tried to clear his head.

He opened the envelope, pulled out the photos of him and Katy again. A strange family washing a car. Is this how they looked to the neighbors? How did Melanie know so much about them? Then he remembered the delinquent car payment notice from the bank, the gray-marbled stationery. *Collections.*

• • •

Phil called a cab and the dispatcher said the underpasses were flooded and he'd have to wait until the water receded. He wrote the bartender a hot check and left.

He walked along the river beside a grove of cotton-woods. He saw a small fire and heard men's low voices, raspy coughing. He and Helen had once seen a shanty along the shore while canoeing. A man's grime-blackened foot jutted from a sleeping bag. Phil started to run, his shoes crunching wet gravel. As the road dipped, he felt cool air against his face. The ground softened underneath him, water seeping into his shoes. The river swelled. He slowed. Water rose over his knees as he slogged through.

Later, at the gate of the festival, he watched the Ferris wheel's revolving lights through the chain-link fence; then the generator quit humming and the wheel darkened. He tucked in his shirt. He walked along the fence to where he could crawl through.

Beer cans, paper plates, banners, leaves, tree limbs. Fallen strings of lights drooping over a kiddie train. Near the music pavilion, plastic chairs were scattered.

He thought of the night before, the bearded man and Helen dancing. Who was he? Phil imagined standing at the kitchen window, years from now, holding Katy's weekend suitcase, watching the bearded man grilling trout on Helen's back porch. On the fridge of Helen's future house, pictures of Helen, Katy and the bearded man bundled in jackets; be-hind them, chalky mountains and cloudless blue sky.

They were all strangers.

A truck loaded with sandbags crawled by.

He walked across the midway on boards stretched across puddles. The sour smell rose again in his nostrils and he thought of the river turning over, rotting sediment rising.

Inside a game booth, a carnie pulled soggy stuffed animals and toys from the shelves, heaved them into boxes. Phil remembered the boxes stacked in his garage. He'd load them into a U-Haul tomorrow, carry them up steep stairs to his new apartment. At night, he'd turn restlessly on the squeaky hide-a-bed, waking to the resiny smell of the fabric softener Helen used on the sheets and pillows.

He stood at the entrance to a video arcade, staring at a coin-operated photo booth, pictures on the front of couples kissing, children holding stuffed animals. Along the walls of the arcade, video games flickered. Squawking electric voices. He looked in the length of mirror on the front of the photo booth. His shoes and pants legs were blackened with river sludge; wet leaves and grass clung to the front of his shirt.

A woman yelled from the back, "You're not supposed to be here. Go on home, now. We're closed."

He wandered out of the arcade, scrambled up an embankment onto a darkened field. He saw the gray outline of the Tilt-A-Whirl. Beyond it shone the Moonwalk. Firemen unloaded sandbags beside the entrance of the festival. Marlina the Oracle's crystal ball and mechanical eye gleamed.

Carnies passed in front of headlights, carrying clothes, TVs, stereo speakers.

In the Moonwalk's plastic window, a child's head bobbed.

"Sir, do you work here?" a fireman asked, shining a flashlight into his face.

"My wife sells tickets. Her name's Helen." Behind the fireman, Phil could see carnies squatting on blankets, sitting on Igloo coolers, their clutter piled around them. Sitting cross-legged on a car hood, a woman in a cowboy hat cradled a man's palm in her hands.

"Your wife, is she missing?"

Phil saw the river's brown waters eddying around the base of ticket booths and food pavilions. Was Helen missing? He thought of her T-shirts, panties, bras, earrings swirling in the current beneath the street, emptying into creeks, moving over worn, pitted limestone, finally joining the swollen river.

He saw himself paddling a canoe between unfamiliar banks, unable to turn against the current.

One of Us Is Hidden Away

"LETTY, I'LL MAKE IT UP TO YOU," REGGIE SAYS TO ME ON the phone like he means it. Only, he's not capable. I clench the receiver with both hands to keep my voice from cracking. "You're pathetic," I say, low and gravelly. I picture him lying there in his bedroom tossing this orange Nerf ball. Flick. His long brown fingers let it go.

"I'm for real. There's this coach coming from St. Edward's," he says.

"This is as serious as your coach," I say. The ball arcs downward, tired and ragged.

"Listen, listen, I want to be a part of it," Reggie says, real urgent. "But next time. Can't they just do this sonic thing next time?" Plastic rim catches the heavy fall.

"Sonogram, Reggie."

"Yeah."

"Jesus. I've told you how the insurance works. Seventh month. Seventh month." My tongue pushes hard at the end of these words. That ball balances on the rim, fat and bloated. Only a second. Then it's in, always.

Reggie goes on awhile about baseball and how it would help him go to college. I say fine. I'm thinking about Cassandra. My dad made her up. He used to tell stories. You'd be riding along and he'd turn off the radio, light a cigarette. "Crack your window, sweetie." And he'd launch into one. Cassandra's a witch. At night she turns into a salamander, sneaking out of her parents' house, crawling down the drainpipe. She meets a lover in the woods. She's not picky—she's in love. The town's afraid of her, though. She knows what'll happen—she's got a sixth sense—but her parents won't listen. One night some of the townspeople set fire to the house. Flames gobble up chunks of roof. She can't find her parents. The townspeople surround the place. Cassandra scoots down the drainpipe, across shoe tops to where her lover's waiting, her slimy skin turning human again. They hold each other in the leaves until it's safe.

"I don't want to screw up school for you." My voice is shaking. Perfect. "But I'm not going through this by myself." It's hot in this kitchen. I'm making some broccoli-cheese soup for my dad. Look at this belly. Ridiculous.

"I'm going to help," Reggie says.

I see him helping, coming up to the hospital after telling his mom Kroger's called him in to stock fruit cocktail and cream corn on the graveyard. Reggie's dark face humming down white corridors. He's moving quick. Shoes squeak as he shuffles. This room, that room. Letty Nen, says so on the card. Inside, all that's left of me is a slight impression on the bedsheet. He can almost make out thighs, ass, maybe some red hairs on the pillow. A baby's where I was.

I'm vanished.

• • •

My dad's a biology teacher at Travis High. Sometimes he comes home and it's like he's still in class, pacing. "Uganda," he says. "I feel like I'm in the goddamn third world. I've got two lousy microscopes. The kids get bored, so they mutilate my frogs. I find this half-frog in the VCR. You can't teach like this. Those were my frogs, Letty."

My dad's got these big hands and they seem to be everywhere at once, opening cabinets, pulling drawers. He stops talking about mutilated frogs and just stands there in the kitchen, like he forgot what he was looking for.

I'm the bent ear. My mom used to be, but she moved. I sit at the table, my feet propped in a chair full of pillows, listening to my dad and chopping onions. I can't quite get past those frogs. In Mexico you see these stuffed frogs in the markets, glazed and stiff, holding miniature guitars and trumpets. Big smiles. Whack.

My dad's a slow eater, separating his plate into neat sections. The lima bean preserve. Acorn squash habitat. He's particular. He'd probably throw up if anything overlapped.

"Reggie wants to go to Dr. Wells's office with me on Thursday," I lie, a goofy-ass smile on my face. He looks up from his squash. His lips have this way of drawing in when he's nervous, like he's got this horrible tasting hunk of food and he's looking for a napkin to spit in.

"He's going to get off his ass and do something? I'll be damned." My dad scratches his chin. "That's great," he says. But behind it are all those words he's plugging up. Like: "Don't trust the fucker."

· · ·

"My breasts leak." I tell Peggy Simon this after my dad hands me the phone.

Peggy says, "Sweetheart, it's just a practice run. Your body's getting ready." In the background, I hear small voices.

Peggy's one of my teachers. She looks like Olive Oyl. Stringy. That's the only way to describe her. She's divorced. We hear all about it in class, how hard it is on your own, her two kids. She's like that. Spills everything.

"I stuffed pieces of toilet paper in my bra. It's embarrassing."

"We'll get you some dress shields, okay? Was that your dad who answered the phone?"

"Yeah, that was Leon."

"How are things? How's he handling the excitement?"

"Okay."

At the table, my dad pours a bowl of cereal and stares at the side of the box. He runs his finger down the list of ingredients. I'm not listening, he's telling me. Go ahead, talk.

"Sometimes I let him feel the baby kick," I say.

Next month I'm going to Houston to visit my mom. She's a stewardess for Mexicana Airlines. My parents separated in October. My dad confides in me that she sleeps around, but I don't think so. She's very private. I just can't see her doing it. Maybe some frustrated guy in Mexico City whose wife's an invalid from the earthquake. It wouldn't bother me much if they could make each other feel better. That's why my dad hid the Beatles albums. He's convinced. He called her a few months back. Red wine gives him a shitty attitude. So he called her in Houston with this attitude that's been building up during Friday Night Videos. No answer. "Whore," he said, right in the middle of a De La Soul video. He just sat there on the couch until he fell asleep with his mouth open.

All these Beatles albums. He hid them. My mom drew these red-ink sketches on the backs. John, Paul, George, Ringo. My dad, he's got them bound up in twine under his bed. I found them while I was vacuuming, back when I could bend over. When she asked him about the albums, he shrugged. "How would I know? I don't keep up with your nostalgia collection, Julie." I haven't told her. I mean, who knows? Maybe my dad needs them more than she does.

I go to this school for pregnant girls. You don't want to go to regular schools like Travis. All they see is this belly, smooth and tight. And it's not welcome at Wendy's or Pancho's Mexican Buffet where everybody eats lunch. So I go to school at St. John's. It's not religious or anything—it's on St. John's Avenue.

Reggie comes by school. We haven't talked in over a week. He comes out on the stage that overlooks the cafeteria, his head tilted back. Reggie's a big dresser—black wool overcoat, pleated slacks. Some of the Mexican girls at the end of my table look up. They draw together close, a mess of mousse-thick hair. He's got this look on his face that's helpless. Who could I possibly know in a place like this? he's thinking. Up on that stage, Reggie's one scared bastard. Dark, high cheekbones like a girl. He wants to be far away. Center field, probably.

The other girls at my table are staring. I'm checking out my peach cobbler, like I don't see him. Reggie's smiling. I can tell before I look up. Lots of teeth. My baby will be born with a full set, grinning.

"Hey Letty," he says, straddling the seat beside me. "This place is something else." He scans the room for a few seconds, then leans forward. "How did the tests go?" He says this as if it's been driving him crazy for days, not knowing. Reggie's head tilts a little. He wants to be a good listener.

I'm about to tell him. About the sonogram, my bent ear, frogs, swollen feet, my mom's albums, the baby's teeth. But I think of Cassandra's sixth sense no one believes. All I say is healthy baby, hundred and sixty-five beats a minute.

"Yeah, well what else?" Reggie asks. "I mean, you get this picture and all, right?" His hands slip down between his knees.

"What do you want me to tell you? Do you want me to describe the picture?" His face tightens up when I say this. I'm squeezing my water bottle. Nothing's left but bubbles.

"No," he says real soft. "No, you tell me what you want, Letty."

Reggie's trying, he is. But I'm not going to let it go. I can feel it tightening up in my throat. "Okay, the baby's white. That's what I saw." I'm kind of amazed how loud I am inside. Everything's vibrating. "Don't worry about breaking the news to your mom because it's not yours."

The assistant principal's eyeing us from the stage. My hand's still squeezing that empty bottle.

"Damn," Reggie says, resettling his butt in the chair. "Why do you have to be this way? I'm doing what's best for both of us." He looks over at the mousse-haired girls. He's acting hurt, his shoulders slumping.

"You chickenshit," I say, but I'm not vibrating anymore. I feel like throwing up.

He says, "Listen, Letty, just for a second. I got the scholarship."

"What does that mean?" I ask. "Are we going to all live together in the dorm?"

Reggie's eyes kind of wobble around, like he can't believe I'm not horny at the prospect of college baseball. "I'm thinking that we'll have weekends," he says. "It'll be like a weekend family, you know?" He looks at me, but focuses on some spot below my eyes.

"Did you tell your mom about your weekend plan, Reggie?"

This stumps him. He rubs a couple of fingers against his temple, not saying anything. I look up and this black girl's bending low over the water fountain against the wall. She's wearing these flimsy pink house slippers. Her feet are too swollen. Nothing else fits.

"I'm waiting for the right time, that's all," Reggie says after a while. Then he says something about things happening too fast. I just nod because I feel sick again. "You look good, Letty. A little rounded and all, but good. Things will work out, you know?" he says, his dark girl-face full of teeth. Then it hits me. I'm going to tell his mom about the baby.

Write her a long letter. Reggie rubs my shoulders and then kisses the top of my head. Those flimsy pink house slippers go swishing by.

It's been two weeks. No call. Nothing. So I call him. The first time I hang up after three rings. The second time Reggie answers. Silence. We're on the line together for a few seconds, but I don't say a thing. "Hey Sam potato-head," he says. "You listening? I'm gonna get you." He hangs up. Sam potato-head. That's what he calls you if you piss him off. If someone tries to pass his Le Mans out on the loop, he'll cut them off, take up two lanes. "Sam fucking potato-head," he'll say. Reggie's a little boy, he really is.

My dad's car is full of rain. Above the windshield, rust-pimples and small holes where the water seeps in. I open the door and the air sticks to my skin, fogs my glasses. Smells like mildew and apples. An inch of water on the floorboard. My dad says parameciums could swim here.

I've got the letter in my hand, thick and serious, like it would make an important change if you read it. Careful, careful, I'm thinking. No return address. I see his mom pulling it from the mailbox with hands that look like his. Long fingers take in the thickness, then open it.

I start up the car, grind gears, and head to the post office. On the way, I see myself watching talk shows, folding tiny clothes, waiting for Reggie to come home for the weekend. There's a sinking in my stomach.

I stall the car twice. The second time, I'm coming down a hill and hear the paramecium water moving toward me from the back. Sounds soft, like a pot boiling. Pooling at my feet. I coast for a few seconds, then settle at the bottom of the hill. The car behind me honks, goes around.

Then my baby's moving. An elbow. Maybe a hand. I suck in. It's hard like a walnut under my fingers. Pushing.

Then it's gone and I breathe.

After a few minutes, a man in a suit knocks on my window. Red veins stand out on his nose. "You okay in there?" he asks.

I roll the window down. "I'm resting," I tell him, narrow my eyes like my mom does when she wants you to go away. He heads back to his Toyota.

I start the car, then creep past the post office, headed home, the letter on the seat beside me.

My dad takes me to Lamaze. It's a little weird going with your dad, sitting on these mats. Everyone's looking us over when we come in. Boyfriends, husbands, girlfriends, wives. What's this old fart doing? they're wondering. Peggy's in the middle of the room, passing out forms. She really lights up when she sees my dad.

"Leon Nen," my dad says, squeezing her hand. All these bellies about to pop, sitting around on mats. A tired pow-wow. Peggy and my dad talk awhile. Peggy leans forward, saying something. Fingers press my dad's shoulder. He laughs, slaps his hands together. He looks happy. Rocking back and forth, one foot, the other.

I'm lying on my mat, thinking about the letter in my purse I didn't send. How something that small can change your life.

In the space between my knees, I see Peggy and Leon, holding everything up. For a few seconds, nothing seems to move. I think of Cassandra in the woods watching her house burn. Except now she's alone in the leaves, no lover. Then Leon uncrosses his arms, and I imagine him putting them around Peggy's skinny waist. Peggy and my dad swaying, feet shuffling, and as they come to the corners of the room, they spin.

There's this pressure on my ribs. Sharp, like someone's got a knitting needle. It catches me by surprise. Some of the women are doing pelvic exercises on their own, rolling what they can, up and down. Not me. Everything's shifting inside. I'm two people, really. One of us is hidden away. But it's all me.

Alias

ON THE FIRST PHONE MESSAGE, LYLE MCKREE HEARD his own tired, flat voice asking his wife Donna if he needed to buy dog food. The second message was from Donna's daughter Sophie. "A fit mother? You're not anybody's mother, bitch."

Lyle rewound the message for Donna to hear. Sophie's baby, Lucy, was asleep in the next room. Lyle and Donna had taken the baby a week earlier while Sophie was at work. Donna had called Coco's to be sure Sophie was on her shift, and they had driven over to the apartment. Bradley, Sophie's boyfriend, was supposed to be watching the baby. Bradley raced bicycles. "Sleeps all day and then he's off on that bike, going God knows where. A sorry situation." That's what the apartment manager had told Donna on the phone. Donna and Lyle had checked up.

When they'd pulled into the apartment parking lot, Lyle noticed fluorescent orange abandoned-car stickers pasted on two car windshields. "Some place," he said.

He and Donna got out, walked up to Sophie's door and knocked. The door opened and Bradley stood in the doorway for a few seconds, rubbing his eyes. He wasn't wearing a shirt. The TV was on and the baby was wailing.

"Sophie's not here," Bradley said, scratching his belly.

"Hear you're not around much either," Lyle said, sharp. Something seemed to catch in his throat. His hands were moist. He looked Bradley over. His arms were tanned up to the shoulders, his calves thick with muscle. His hairless legs were as brown and smooth as polished wood.

"You are a nasty man, aren't you?" Bradley said, wagging a finger. "Get on home nasty man." He grinned and then glanced back to where the baby was.

"Listen smartass," Donna had said, pushing by Bradley into the living room, "we know all about you leaving this child." Bending over, she lifted the baby out of the playpen.

Bradley started to close the door, but Lyle wedged his shoulder between door and frame. For a few seconds, Bradley squeezed the door against him and Lyle could feel Bradley's breath.

"I don't remember inviting *you*," Bradley said.

Lyle shoved his way in. He balled his fists and moved toward Bradley. Bradley shuffled his feet like a boxer and pretended to take a swing. Lyle's hands went up. "Ha," Bradley said, smirking, putting his hands down at his sides. "Could've had you." Lyle's heart hammered in his chest. For a second, nobody moved. The baby was crying in Donna's arms. Lyle noticed the apartment had a mildewed smell. He stepped over a pile of clothes to gather some of the baby's things. A red touring bike hung upside down from brackets in the ceiling. He pictured Bradley bent over it, legs churning. Lyle wondered if Bradley ever biked near his insurance office. He imagined ramming Bradley with his car, Bradley's body thumping across the hood.

The baby was red-faced and furious, climbing Donna's chest.

"We're filing charges. I'll let you know that right now, son," Lyle had said, moving a paper bag to the side. There was a wet circle on the carpet underneath it. Lyle's jaw hardened. "Goddamn but this place is filthy."

"Tell me something, Lyle. Sophie says you used to come into her room naked at night. That true?"

"I've got a gun," Lyle heard himself saying. "Don't come near this baby again." His face felt hot. Donna's hand touched his shoulder.

Lyle and Donna peeled shrimp at the kitchen table, while Lucy sat in her high chair gnawing bread crust. Lyle sniffed the thawing coffee can. The shrimps inside were gray lumps. "Been in the freezer too long," he said.

"We'll have to make that trip again. Lucy can play in the ocean." Donna ran her fingers through Lucy's thin hair. "I'll buy a little shovel and pail. We'll hunt for sand dollars, won't we, dumpling?"

Lyle thought about a motel in Rockport where he and his son, Robbie, once stayed. It had a long pier, and he and Robbie had gone crabbing. He saw his son, bird-legged, gawky, his hair long and blond under his Astros cap. That was when Robbie spent a month out of every summer with him. They'd lure the crabs with chicken wings tied with string. The crabs looked larger on the sandy bottom than on the pier.

Now Robbie lived with his mother and, except for Christmas, the visits had stopped. Lyle had slipped up. Two summers before there had been a party at a neighbor's house, and in-between Trivial Pursuit games, Lyle had seen Robbie and Robbie's friend Jimmy Gould stealing sips from unattended drinks. And later, Jimmy Gould's older brother poured them beers and he saw that too. He said nothing, remembering his own father's liquor cabinet and how his father marked the bottles with a wax pen to keep track. Late in the evening, when one of the women tried to teach Robbie to dance to George Strait, Robbie had stumbled, then slumped down in a chair, and threw up on himself. "I'm dizzy," he said, pulling at the front of his vomit-slickened shirt. "Don't tell Mom I'm dizzy, okay?" Lyle had taken off Robbie's clothes and then lowered him into the shower. The rank smell of him made Lyle gag, and as he studied the acne down Robbie's back, he felt a sudden revulsion toward his son that made him ashamed. "Morally bankrupt," his ex-wife had said. Somehow she had pried the story out of Robbie. "You were right there in the house. Any man who'd let his son drink himself sick needs to reevaluate." Where would he start? he'd wondered at the time.

Now, Lyle didn't know his son anymore, didn't know if he dated girls with bad complexions, smoked clove cigarettes, or still liked to read Isaac Asimov novels. Things he should know. It had occurred to Lyle that much of his life had passed. He'd be out of town on insurance business, stretched out on a motel bed, watching a pay-per-view, and these thoughts would come to him. He'd pick up the phone, weigh it in his hand.

Lyle heard something thump against the roof, then off the back of the house.

"What the hell was that?" he said. He moved to the sliding glass door, opened it. A rock skipped off the patio. Another clanged off the barbecue. Annie, their border collie, was running along the wooden fence, barking. Lyle could hear rustling behind the fence. Feet on gravel. Voices. He stood on a fence rung, looked over. A boy in a red shirt disappeared over a neighbor's fence. Lyle went back inside. "Just some kids," he said.

"Maybe we ought to get the police to look into that too," Donna said.

"Our plate's plenty full," Lyle said. "They already send that patrol car around."

"Why don't I feel safe then?"

Lyle sat down at the table. He rubbed his temples.

"Look at this child. How could anybody do what he did?" Donna shook her head. She tickled Lucy, who frowned. "It gives me the willies."

"Who knows what might have happened if we hadn't done something," Lyle said, peeling and then tossing a shrimp into a bowl. His hands were cold.

"We probably don't even know the worst of it. That place reeked of pot."

"Was that what it was?" Lyle said, pulling Lucy from the high chair. She squealed and pinched the skin of his neck.

"My daughter calls me 'bitch' now," Donna said suddenly, as if answering some question put to her.

"Sophie doesn't know what she's doing." That was all Lyle could think of to say. He imagined grabbing Sophie by her dark roots, getting in her face, asking what the hell was she thinking.

"We did the right thing, didn't we Lyle?"

"Sure."

Lyle squeezed lemon juice on his fingers, rubbed them together. He thought about the crabs, the tight, pinched feel of sunburned skin, he and Robbie, heads bent over the pier, watching their blue shells rising through the kelp.

Around 3:30 in the morning Lyle scrambled for the phone. Rock music blared from the other end. Guitars screamed feedback. Lyle ran a hand through his hair and then unplugged the cord.

"Good God. Who was that?" Donna asked.

"Mr. Funnybones."

"Who?"

"A crank call."

"Well, what did they say?" Donna's face tightened. She sat up in bed.

"Nothing." Lyle crawled into the bed, pulling the sheet over himself. In the room down the hall the baby began to cry. "Shit. Whose turn is it?"

"Was it Bradley?"

"I don't know. Maybe it was." Lyle looked at her. "Probably not." His bare feet touched the carpet. He slipped on his robe and walked down the hall toward the baby's room. The night light painted his feet yellow. They were bony, ugly feet. His first wife had told him that his toes never touched the ground when he walked, that his toes waved. "Bye-bye toes," she would say.

Lifting Lucy out of the crib, Lyle held her against his chest. He rocked side to side, humming in a low voice. After a while her crying became small spasms, and she loosened her grip on his robe. He remembered Robbie having colic. His first wife smelling like baby powder, nudging him awake. Walking the floor, Robbie thrashing in the crook of his arm, stroking Robbie's belly. The cold bathroom tile under his feet. Half asleep, pissing.

Over his shoulder, in the mirror, he saw his shaven face, which had become rounded and jowly beneath the beard that covered it for ten years. Thin grooves wandered from the corners of his eyes. Under one ear, two small cuts where he'd nicked himself with the razor the day before. There was a custody hearing in a week. "Shave it. They might wonder what you're hiding under that beard." Donna had tugged the gray shag of his chin, giggled. "Do you have an alias, Mr. McKree?"

With his free hand Lyle cleared a space in the crib for the baby. For a few moments he watched the slight rise and fall of her chest. He thought of the train trip to Copper Canyon that he and Donna planned for the upcoming summer. She'd called it their getaway. They hadn't had enough of those in their life, she said.

Once when Lyle was in college, he'd taken a twenty-one-hour train ride to Acapulco. He had a window seat and didn't sleep a wink, being in a strange place, not speaking the language, the train winding over dark gorges.

Donna and Lyle took the baby to the park. Small trees were scattered around and dust swirled off the playground. The edges of the sky were hazy-brown.

Women dressed in sweat pants and T-shirts stood near the swing sets, talking, watching their children. They looked at Lyle, who was carrying Lucy on his hip over to a picnic table. They went on talking. The women were in their twenties. One of them had on a T-shirt that said Cowboy Junkies. Dark braided hair hung down her back. Her sweat pants were drawn up to a spot just above her knees, showing her calves. He thought of his first wife when she was young, straddling a bike in her swimsuit. They'd been drinking at a friend's pool party and she'd accused him of making a pass at one of the women. He followed her around the side of the house. "I nibbled at her shoulder," he pleaded, standing in the friend's front yard. "It was a joke." But the moment he'd said it, he knew it was a lie. That he'd risked everything he valued—his marriage, his son, his friends—and it hadn't fazed him. In the streetlight, his first wife's bare back and shoulders shone white as bone. "You're drunk," he said to her. "Come on back inside. It's not safe riding around like that." He walked across the yard, put a hand to her shoulder, and she shook him off. She screamed at him. "I'm not drunk! Do I look drunk?"

"Cowboy Junkies," Lyle told Donna in the park. "What kind of name is that?" Donna was digging through a sack of sandwiches and chips they brought from home. In the summer she sometimes wore pantyhose with shorts to hide her varicose veins.

"We need to meet other couples," Donna said, pulling out a graham cracker and giving it to Lucy, who squealed and jabbered. After a few seconds, Lucy threw the cracker on the ground.

The wind kicked up, sending paper and dust spinning across the dry grass. He took a bite from his sandwich and looked out on the playground. He imagined the dust sifting through his skin, fine pink powder settling quietly in between joints, bone, filling body cavities.

Hardening.

Lyle sat in his Celica at the back of the apartment parking lot. It was dusk and the sky was streaked with purple. He'd been there for over an hour filming the comings and goings of the apartment with a video camera. Bradley was squatting with a flashlight near the dumpster, unfolding a large, transparent bag. His hands moved methodically inside and outside the billowing bag until it was too dark for Lyle to see. After a while Bradley struck a match and candlelight flickered inside the bag. Small flames spread until it shone like a lantern. Along the border of the light Lyle could see Bradley's face. The bag filled with hot air, swayed in the breeze. He looks happy. That's what Lyle was thinking as it began to rise slowly over the parking lot, the apartments, the tops of trees. A man with a trash can stood and stared. Lyle pointed his camera.

• • •

"Hallucinogenic mushrooms," Donna said from the bathtub. "That's what kids are into at the university. My friend Brenda works in the registrar's office and she hears a lot about what goes on in the dorms."

They'd watched the video of Bradley and the fire balloon together, though Lyle had hesitated when she asked to see it. "Parts are out of focus," he'd said. "You can't see much." He wondered now why he said this.

"Kids do sick stuff on those things," Donna continued.

"We really don't know what went on. It's just speculation," Lyle said, his voice stiff.

"Speculation? Lyle, you know how weak-willed Sophie is. Mentally, she's a child."

Lyle heard Donna's body squeak against the tub bottom. Later she would crawl out and want him to give her a massage before going to sleep, her body sprawled forward on the bed, skin warm and pliant under his fingers. He thought of his first wife, the soft edges of her face, dark eyebrows. She would ask him for a glass of wine before she nursed Robbie. It made them both sleep better, she said.

"We should make an anonymous call." Donna opened the drain, and the water gurgled.

"What would we say?"

"That he's on something. That he's dangerous. Suppose that balloon thing lands on somebody's roof?"

"It won't."

"But suppose?"

• • •

It was late. The baby was awake and running a fever. Donna asked Lyle if he wouldn't mind driving up to Albertson's for Tylenol.

Lyle backed the Celica out of the driveway. Most of the houses on their street were dark. Between streetlights, Lyle could see hazy patches of stars. A couple of kids were sitting in a parked LeSabre farther down the street. Small flickers of light appeared behind the windows.

Lyle turned onto an access road and punched the accelerator. He rolled down the window and the cold air rushed in, scattering file folders on the back seat. The skin on his neck and face tingled. He leaned his head out the window, and the wind roared around him. He yelled but couldn't hear himself, only felt the vibration of his voice. His eyes watered until he couldn't see the road.

"She's got Sophie's small mouth," Donna said, smearing sunscreen onto Lucy's face. "And if you look at her pinkies, you can see Granddaddy Lewis's crook. We all have it."

Lyle filled a kiddie pool with water. He could feel the heat rising from the lawn. The sky was blue and cloudless. Next door he could hear a baseball game on a radio.

"You remember any redheads in your family? What was that character's name?" Lyle said.

"Ugh." Donna wrinkled her nose. "Bradley's not my side—more like yours. Watch her while I get my suit on."

Donna gave Lucy a cranberry juice–filled bottle and walked over, pulled back the sliding glass door and went inside.

Lyle picked up the video camera and found Lucy in the viewer, crawling. She immediately stuck a fistful of leaves and dirt into her mouth. "Don't eat that crap." He pulled them out with his fingers and she began to cry, her tongue blackened by dirt. He gave her the lens cap and she stuck it in her mouth. He watched her sit up and tumble sideways. There was no breeze and he was starting to sweat. Next door, the announcers talked excitedly as someone hit a double.

The custody hearing was a week away and Lyle wondered if they might be able to come to some agreement beforehand. He saw Bradley in the courtroom dressed in a suit, his smirk giving the world the finger, not knowing what was at stake. Then, it struck him: Bradley and Sophie wouldn't show up. His shoulders tightened.

He was sipping his beer when the rocks came over the fence. A few small ones landed in the grass near him, others banged off the shed roof. Kids laughing. Feet crunching gravel.

Lyle moved toward the fence but remembered the baby and reversed himself, staring at the grass where she had been. He saw Donna inside the house, wild-eyed, fumbling with the sliding glass door. In the baby pool, Lucy lay on her side, her head beneath the water. When he pulled her from the pool she spasmed and coughed and flailed her arms, beating his face and neck, her mouth gaping silently. He held her to his chest. She began to wail. On the grass beside his feet, Donna's shadow rose. Then Lyle felt his legs slacken as if giving way to some tremendous weight.

New Years

On New Year's Eve, Margaret's ex-husband David was supposed to pick up their son Tim for dinner. David told her he'd made a seven o'clock reservation at an expensive Italian restaurant downtown, where he and Margaret had celebrated their final anniversary. His girlfriend Lena would be with him, but Margaret didn't allow her in the house.

Margaret watched snow slant through the porch light, thinking she could count on David being thirty minutes late for everything. Years ago, he'd made her late for her best friend's wedding. Afterwards, Margaret had been furious, though she'd said nothing, only gotten drunk on champagne at the reception. Later, after he'd had to clasp her around the waist and half-drag her to the car, she lay on the back seat, unable to stop saying how sorry she was. The next morning, she found she'd bitten the inside of her cheek.

An explosion echoed off the front porch. Margaret didn't move. Tim's stereo thumped from his room. Then she went to the front door, opened it. Cold, wet air. She stepped outside. In the snow-coated flower bed lay a blackened bottle rocket. She picked it up, wondering if one of Tim's friends had launched it. She went back inside, set the bottle rocket on the kitchen table. She grabbed an open bottle of Chardonnay from the fridge, poured a large glass, and drank it down.

That September, Tim and his friend Robert had vandalized the elementary school a few blocks from Margaret's house. They'd climbed in through the roof maintenance door, blown up an aquarium with homemade explosives, torched artwork and blackened walls with aerosol cans and Bic lighters. Alarms sounded. Sprinklers soaked the carpet. Margaret remembered the phone ringing in the dark, fumbling for it, her heart thudding, the police officer's voice saying *Your son's here with us Mrs. Odom. We've got him.*

Now, Margaret thought of calling David, asking if the dinner had slipped his mind. But she was afraid Lena might answer. Once, she'd heard Lena's voice on David's answering machine, reading what he later explained was part of a poem: *I have eaten the plums that were in the icebox and which you were probably saving for breakfast—forgive me and please leave a message.*

Margaret had hung up.

Tim came into the kitchen wearing a suit Margaret bought at a men's resale shop two days before. The jacket sleeves were too long, halving his hands. She'd had to guess at the sleeve length because Tim wouldn't go with her. Tim was fourteen, tall and lanky like his father, but his shoulders were childlike, disproportionate. "This suit's a piece of crap," he said.

"Your friends sent you a present," Margaret said, pointing to the bottle rocket.

Tim glanced at it, shrugged.

The phone rang and Margaret picked it up.

"Margaret, this is Lena," a tight voice said.

"Where's David?" Margaret said sharply.

"Stuck in the door," Lena said, her voice tilting. "His pants are caught on the weather stripping."

"What?" Margaret said. She watched Tim pick up the bottle rocket off the kitchen table, examine it.

Lena said, "He might be dead. I'm not sure. He fell in the snow. He hit his head, on the driveway. He was just lying out there. I pulled him up the steps. I called an ambulance."

Silence.

"Lena?"

"Yes."

"Is he breathing?" Margaret asked.

The phone clattered. Margaret could hear Lena in the background, saying, David? David? Margaret imagined his legs jutting onto a strange porch, snow settled in the folds of his pants. Beside the door, large glazed pots gleamed.

"I want this to stop," Lena said harshly into the phone.

Ten months ago, David had left Margaret and moved in with Lena, a part-time art teacher at the high school where David taught history. "It's not some fling," he'd told Margaret on the phone after pretending to be at a history teacher conference in Memphis. "Lena has this passion for people, ideas."

David talked about the sudden turn his life had taken.

Margaret imagined his scribbled notes on a pad beforehand. *Don't forget the part about it being nobody's fault, victims of circumstance.*

"When did all this happen?" Margaret asked, her voice rising. For a few seconds, David was quiet. Then he said, "You had to have known."

What was there to know? She'd thought of the previous summer's faculty retreat, women she'd marked after her third glass of wine as *interested*. David had introduced her to Lena, whose henna-dyed hair and black leotard under cut-offs had caused Margaret to dismiss her then. "I'm teaching David ceramics during his off-period," Lena said when David went to grab silverware. Margaret had wondered then how much of David's day, which she'd always imagined filled with paperwork and student discipline problems, was inaccessible to her.

Standing in the buffet line, Lena was loud and her pale hands gestured wildly when she talked. Margaret had fixed Lena in her late twenties. She'd noticed a small green snake tattooed beneath Lena's bra strap when Lena raised her arm and remembered how this kind of affectation normally irritated David. "Half my advanced class has piercings and tattoos—where's the rebellion in that?" he'd once told her. Staring at the melon balls, Margaret had a difficult time pairing Lena and David in her mind and relaxed a little. They talked about Tim's school problems, his apathy.

"Tim and I should talk sometime," Lena had said. "I'm super with kids."

• • •

In the hospital waiting room, the doctor approached Margaret and Lena. "E. B. Gordon," he said, squatting in front of them. His black hair was slicked back and his eyes were red and puffy. His shirt was wrinkled as though he'd slept in it. Earlier, when Margaret had gotten off the elevator looking for Lena, she had seen the doctor in the corner of the waiting room holding an old woman's hand—now he took Margaret's hand in between his large ones. He looked from Margaret to Lena. "Which of you—"

"David lives with me," Lena said.

Gordon let go of Margaret's hand, shifted his feet, faced Lena. "David's had an aneurysm—a hemorrhaging in one of the arteries in his brain."

Lena folded her arms over her stomach, the zippers on the sleeves of her leather jacket tinkling.

In a corner of the waiting room a TV glowed. A crowd stood in Times Square bundled in jackets and scarves, waving.

"We've been having fights," Lena said, turning to Dr. Gordon. "Can stress cause these things?"

"I could tell you stress might be a factor, but what good would it do?" Dr. Gordon rubbed his eyes with his fingers. "We carry these flaws with us. There's no predicting when they'll rupture."

Lena began sobbing. Margaret looked out the window at car headlights passing below. She would have to leave for her shift at the counseling center soon and work until four A.M. Around the holidays, most of the men and women who called the crisis hotline wanted to talk about their children.

I worry about them forgetting me, they'd say, or *Why don't they call?* Sometimes they described their children in such detail, Margaret pictured fingers pinching wallet snapshots, shoulders slumping. It seemed to her they preferred these static children to their real ones. Some nights she wondered if she and David had become like these parents, disembodied, abstract.

"I know I've been a little scarce," David had told her after their meeting with Tim's probation officer just before Thanksgiving. "But in the spring he can stay as long as he wants. We'll build a kiln together in the backyard."

"He'll be in reform school by then," Margaret had snapped.

"There's no need for panic," David had said. "Tim's just testing limits."

"How about you?" she'd asked.

In the waiting room, Margaret turned to Lena and told her David would get through this. But there was a detached sound to her voice. Did she sound like this to callers at work? She looked at Lena's red cowboy boots, her braided rope of henna hair. Under Lena's eyes, mascara ran. Lena seemed years younger, a child.

Dr. Gordon stood across from them, talking to a family sitting near the pay phones. A woman with cropped red hair dropped her head, stared at the carpet, a gesture that reminded Margaret of the first time David and Lena brought Tim home after a weekend together, and Margaret, watching from the porch, had seen Lena's tinted face in the car window, staring at something in her lap. "Dad's a moron," Tim had told Margaret while carrying a duffel bag inside the house. Tim said Lena had given him a pair of paint-spattered overalls. "You wear them without a shirt for effect," Tim had said, imitating Lena. "Jackson Pollock." Tim tossed them. "She smells like an ashtray," he said to Margaret. "What's Dad thinking?"

"People find out things too late," Margaret said, wondering if she had.

For months after that, Margaret thought of Tim as an ally. In the afternoon, Tim would call Margaret at the counseling center. "Mom? I'm at Vulcan's," he'd mumble, video games squawking. Sometimes when she came home, she'd find tuna melts or fish sticks wrapped in foil in the fridge. He'd even helped her dig a plot for a fall garden. For a while she imagined Tim had stepped into the void David left.

But just after Thanksgiving, Tim had stopped calling. He was nearly always gone when she came home at nine. She spent her off-hours calling his friends' parents, asking for him. Then, Margaret had gone through Tim's backpack one night and found PVC pipe and copper wire. She'd shattered the pipe with her car tire and tossed the fragments on his bed, telling him if he pulled another goddamn stunt, he could go live in his father's art colony.

In the waiting room, one of the pay phones rang and Margaret stiffened, then stood up and answered it. "Call for the Bates family," she said in a loud voice, and an old man in a baseball cap rose near the water fountain, nodded and took the phone.

Dr. Gordon came over and led Lena and Margaret to a small room near the nurses' station and explained how he'd use a clip to stop the artery's bleeding. He showed them the

CAT scan of David's brain. Gray arteries branched like ten-drils, an inverted root. In the bend of one artery, a shadow. Margaret thought of David's young face in one of her wedding photos. He had long sideburns and a wide-lapel tux and was climbing into their shaving-creamed Camaro, one leg suspended, his face turned toward the camera, a cocky smile. Posing confident. His brain carried the aneurysm's seed even then.

She wondered if the end of their marriage, its arbitrary breaking apart, was hidden, like the aneurysm, in the ordinary folds of their past—a forgotten telephone message, a change in someone's tone of voice, the silences in their love-making.

In her mind, David's face blurred, became Tim's. He sat at home, his suit rumpled now, watching the year-end music video countdown. When she had headed out, keys in hand, saying your dad's in the hospital, he's hurt, Tim refused to come. He pulled at his tie. But the muscles of his jaw tight-ened. Under the harsh kitchen light, the stove and refriger-ator seemed ridiculously clean. Margaret moved across the room to hold him, but his arms hung at his sides, his body leaning backward. A hardness rose in Margaret's chest. She wanted to slap him.

Once, when Tim was three, Margaret had left him in the front seat of their station wagon and had gone back inside for her checkbook. Tim had put the car into neutral, and as the car rolled backwards down the drive, sunlight gleaming off chrome, Margaret stood at the front door watching his head grow small in the distance.

She felt Tim slipping from her now, as David had. *You had to have known.*

Margaret looked at Dr. Gordon's puffy eyes and tried to imagine them straining as they stared at David on the examination table, seeing past skin, bone, milky tissue to what was wrong.

Later, Margaret watched Lena on the pay phone talking to David's mother, Valerie, in California. Lena spoke quietly, winding and unwinding the phone cord around her hand. Margaret wondered how often they talked, and if David and Lena had lied to her about their living arrangement. Margaret pictured Valerie opening her own front door, getting a look at her prospective daughter-in-law, the old woman's drooping jaw. Valerie had stepped through their front door on New Year's Day, years ago, right after Margaret and David married. David hid the bourbon and a few bottles of un-opened champagne in a cabinet above the stove because Valerie didn't tolerate drinking. They held hands, said grace and then Margaret got up to get the lasagna from the oven. There was a loud pop. Champagne gushed from the cabinet above her head, streaming, hissing over the oven. Valerie glared at Margaret. Then she folded her napkin in front of her and mouthed a silent prayer, the ghosts of words.

But since the divorce, Valerie had started calling Margaret and they'd talked about David's infrequent visits with Tim and Margaret's adjustments, her new life. "I think of you as my daughter," Valerie had said a few weeks ago. "That's a funny thing to say at this point, I know. You can't choose your children, can you?" Margaret didn't know. Their new intimacy seemed born out of mutual disappointment; each was now reconciled to less.

In the waiting room, Lena slumped to the floor sobbing, the pay phone receiver dangling above her head. Margaret hung up the phone and helped her back to a chair. Lena's hands fluttered, then reached for her. For a moment, a feeling of revulsion seized Margaret and she felt her stomach tighten. She held Lena loosely, smelling the ashy odor of her skin.

"I'm so glad you're here," Lena said, sniffing. Her face was smeared with mascara.

Margaret said, "It's a hard time," took a Kleenex from her purse, wiped the mascara from Lena's cheeks. She glanced down at her own blouse, looking for smudges.

In a while, Margaret imagined, David's friends would show up, some of whom she had known her whole adult life; she'd attended their wives' baby showers, children's birthdays. Now they would acknowledge her quietly, bring casseroles and flowers for Lena. Margaret's throat tightened.

A nurse with a pillow under each arm came into the room and dimmed the lights. In the corner, a late night talk show flickered silently. Strings of firecrackers popped in the distance.

Across the room, a family sprawled on a couch, asleep. Kids' toys, a Scrabble game, and a pizza box lay on the floor in front of them. A blond girl rested her head on her mother's lap. Margaret heard the mother moaning softly. Her husband whispered, rubbed her shoulders until she returned to sleep.

"I need to go," Margaret told Lena. She wanted to call Tim, hear his voice. "Someone covered the first half of my shift—but I need to be there."

"Sure," Lena said, nodding, squeezing Margaret's hand. "I completely understand." She bent over, reached into her shoulder bag, pulled out a pack of cigarettes. She looked at Margaret. "I know the past ten months have been rough," she said quickly, her eyes jumping from Margaret to the cigarette then to the sprawled family across the room. "They haven't been easy on David either."

Margaret didn't say anything. She felt a tiredness settle into her legs and hips.

Lena smiled nervously. She stuffed her cigarettes back in her bag, turned and disappeared through the ICU door. Margaret listened to her boots clomp down the hallway.

She picked up the phone and called Tim. The answering machine clicked on and she heard her own voice sounding ridiculously calm. . . . *and we promise to get back to you soon as we can.* "Tim, where are you?" she said after the beep. "Your dad keeps asking about you," she lied. Then, a squall, Tim's voice underneath saying hello hello.

"Would you like me to come get you?" Margaret asked.

"What does he look like?" Tim said, sleepily.

"He's the same old dad. He's got a good-size lump on his head though," she said, hating his half-awake voice, the careless way it diminished things. "An artery is leaking in his brain." She'd wanted him to cry; she wanted him to see how breakable they were.

"Does he know who we are?"

Margaret heard mumbling like someone was trying to

talk with a mouth full of food. "Who's at the house, Tim? Is that Robert?"

"Nobody's here Mom, all right?" She heard echoes of David's voice in his irritation. Blood thudded in her head, and she saw her own dark, branching arteries.

Margaret took the elevator down, got in her car, and pulled onto the snow-packed road, headed to the counseling center. She rose onto the overpass and crept along in third gear, grainy flakes whirling through the headlights. Below, in the streetlight's orange glare, she could see snow-shrouded roofs, driveways, yards.

The nurse had said she'd call them if there was a change in David's condition and Margaret felt relieved not to have to depend on Lena. Earlier, Lena had pulled David's wallet from her purse, taken out his license, held it in her palm. "She means if he's not all there," Lena had said, "his head lolling, mumbling gobbledygook."

Margaret drove another half-mile before she noticed her fingers ached from gripping the wheel. When she was small, she would ride in her father's car and pretend they had no brakes—she'd close her eyes, brace her legs against the front seat, a wild faith in her ability to make things stop.

"It's a strange dream," the male caller said into the phone.

"You mean disturbing?" Margaret asked.

"Yes. But comforting too. My son Chris died thirty-five years ago. I delivered him. I was an obstetrician. Unwound the umbilical from his throat. That is a weighty thing—to hold that cord before it's cut. We buried it under a plum tree in the backyard. The dried umbilical, I mean."

"Your son died."

"Yes. He was seven. That's the way I see him in the dream, he's always seven, with burred blond hair. He used to keep snapping turtles in an above-ground pool in the backyard and he had a string belt beaded with dragonfly heads. It's funny what you remember." He paused. "Do you have children?"

"Yes. A boy—fourteen."

"I guess you know then." He cleared his throat. "The night it happened, we were delivering Christmas gifts to relatives around town. Chris was in the back seat smacking gum. A drunk had fallen asleep at a stop sign and I honked at him and went around. At the next stop sign he comes up behind me, blaring his horn and pulls up against my bumper: I felt him pushing. I remember seeing him in the rearview. He had a flabby chin. He popped the clutch—probably by accident—and sent us lurching forward. No one should've been hurt—it wasn't even enough force to move the presents off the seat. I asked Chris if he was okay and he didn't answer. I opened the back door, crawled onto the seat over him, patted his cheek. He wasn't breathing. I pulled a wad of gum out of his teeth, gave him mouth-to-mouth. The drunk was screaming you son of a bitch, but, after he saw what I was doing, he quit. I was pounding on Chris's chest." The caller paused. There was a soft buzzing on the line. "Later I remember seeing bruises there."

"You tried to save him," Margaret said.

"Yes. I tried." He paused again. "We found out later that he had a golf-ball-size tumor pressing against his heart. Blood flow had slowed—he'd probably had circulation problems in his hands and feet. His heart was working overtime. In any case, it had quit the moment the drunk hit us."

"What about the dream?" Margaret asked.

"In the dream, I'm old, older than I am now and Chris walks toward me through the backyard gate of our old house. I can smell freshly cut grass. Hear cicadas. Chris's umbilical is still connected, a loose end looped over his arm. He kisses me. Then he runs over to his turtle pool, stands on the ladder and pees into it."

"You have this dream all the time?" Margaret asked.

"Once a week at least." He paused. "It's unsettling. But it feels good too."

When Margaret pulled into her driveway, the New Year was nearly four hours old. It had stopped snowing and gotten colder. From the thick-layered cars she guessed six inches had fallen. In the distance hung a bank of rust-stained clouds.

The house was dark. She opened her car door and stood in the muffled quiet of the street, wondering if Tim was home. She went inside, pulled her coat off and put some water on the stove for herbal tea. David's surgery was at seven. She thought of Dr. Gordon's puffy eyes, David being packed in ice to lower his body temperature, his heart rate slowing. Hibernation. What happened when he thawed?

Splayed over the back of the couch were the gray suit

jacket and pants she'd bought for Tim. A shed skin. Tim lay curled on his side, an afghan bunched around him. There was no sign of Robert. She bent over him. The smell of soured wine, smoke. Where had he been?

The kettle whistled. She went to the stove, poured a cup of tea, then wandered into the living room. She pulled a photo album from the shelf, opened it, turned vinyl sheets. Nursing Tim in the hospital bed, her face pale, exhausted. She could remember fragments of her C-section, mostly whirring, sucking sounds, the mechanics. But she couldn't remember Tim being pulled from her body and this irritated her. Where had those seconds gone?

She turned the page. In another photo, her father was holding Tim, kissing his bald head.

She remembered her father spinning her by the arms in their front yard when she was small. Mailbox, bay windows, roses, his parked Buick, crape myrtles. Drunken spinning. She had felt deliriously happy. Smiling creases under her father's chin.

On another page, David stood next to the hospital bed, hamming, a rose in his teeth, stubble shadowing his cheeks. He used to tell her jokes. *A snowman goes to see his doctor for some tests. Next day, the doctor calls him up, says, hey, good news: those lumps we found were only coal.*

Tim breathed heavily on the couch.

She sipped the hot tea, then moved to the couch and pulled the afghan over Tim's shoulders. His half-grown face, slack jaw. At the hospital, Lena would be next to David's bed, her pale, childlike hand clasping his.

• • •

It was still dark when the clock radio woke her at six A.M. Margaret pulled on her robe, wandered to the bathroom, and pinned up her hair in the mirror. She was scrubbing her face with Noxzema when the explosion rattled the windows. A sound like snapping sheet metal.

The front door opened and slammed shut, Tim's shoes squeaking on the tile. He was breathing hard. Outside, car alarms blared.

"What did you do?" she yelled at him from the hallway. Then something broke in her chest and she put her hands over her face.

The heater clicked on.

Tim wiped his nose, sniffed. His cheeks red from the cold.

"What did you do?" she said again, her voice softening. She looked at him between her fingers.

"They're coming out to see what it was," he said. He ran to the kitchen, took a flashlight from the drawer. "No one saw me." Tim stood still, flicked the flashlight on and off.

Margaret looked out the porch window. It was snowing again. Indistinct figures bundled in jackets tracked through the yards, their flashlight beams slanting over unbroken whiteness. Soon the police would arrive, ask questions about the explosion. What would she say?

Her hand grew cold against the window. A vapor outlined it.

The car alarms blared on.

At the hospital later, Lena would reach for her. They would all wait together.

"Pretend, okay?" Tim said, helping her with her jacket.

She slipped on her boots and then opened the door. They stepped out, their white breath streaming in the porch light.

Worry

MY BROTHER'S BLOOD WAS A SHADOW ON THE GROUND making my stomach grab. I stood in the near-dark vacant lot, knowing I'd meant to hit Michael with the baseball. He thought Dad had come back to us, when he hadn't. I'd seen Dad and the woman in her kitchen window, their hard-pressing bodies. Dad looked up and saw me. Then, in the vacant lot, telling Michael, one more pitch, right about here. Michael on the ground, screaming, his shadowy blood on the dirt. But the longer I stood there, the more hitting him seemed only bad luck.

It was hot. I wiped my face on the front of my T-shirt. Dad's shoes slapped over the street, then swished through weeds to where we were. Michael was doubled-up on the ground. Blood-gooped hands cupped his face. "Jesus," Dad said, his face flimsy and blue in the half-light. "What the hell happened?" He crouched down, already knowing what I'd done, but making it an accident because it was easier.

I said, "Michael didn't get his glove up in time." In the

air my hand tracing my hard-ass line drive that put Michael on the ground. "Thunk," I said. I was still holding the bat.

Dad said, "It's goddamn dark out. What are you using for brains, Andrew?"

On the ground, Michael made a soup-slurping sound. Then moaned, soft. Across the street, I saw the woman standing under the porch light, her skinny arms folded tight, like they might fly off. Her face was shiny. Dad had told us he was building her a house, that they had to go over floor plans.

In the vacant lot, Dad chewed his lip and squatted down beside Michael. Then he said, "Stay still, son," quiet, like he'd better not fuck this up, or Mom would start getting into the wrong cars at Foodland again. He patted Michael's shoulder, then pulled Michael's hands away from the mess. Michael moaned. I looked at the outline of trees at the back of the lot. Dad told me to take off my shirt and I said why and he said, just do it, Andrew. I pulled it over my head. He yanked it from me, wadded it against Michael's nose, and told him to tilt his head back. He helped Michael onto wobbly legs and they started across the street, Dad's arm around his waist. Michael staring up at the sky, like a saint on one of those prayer cards Mrs. Arceneaux used to give us at church. *St. Anthony, patron saint of lost objects, help us in our petition.*

Streetlights flicked on.

With the bat, I knocked a rock into the trees and then followed Dad and Michael across the street. Nickel-size blood drops made a trail on the cement. I scuffed a couple with my shoe. I found the baseball near the curb and picked it up. Dad looked back at me from the driveway. I held the ball up, like naming bad luck.

"You coming?" Dad asked.

"Where?"

"What do you mean where? The hospital." Dad helped Michael into the truck. Michael mumbled something underneath my wadded shirt.

"It's not that bad, is it?" I said.

Dad stared at me. "What's wrong with you?"

I shrugged.

The woman came out of the house with a baggie full of ice and handed it to Dad. Her eyes were red like she'd been crying. "This is Carla," Dad said, stiff. She nodded at me, then looked back at Dad. "Is he going to be all right?" she asked.

"It busted his nose," Dad said, quiet, then leaned into the truck with the ice, and said something to Michael.

It looked like Carla was about to say something too, but she didn't. One of her hands fidgeted around her mouth, then she pinned her arms to her chest like before. I could tell she wanted us gone, like she knew we were going to cost her something if we stayed another minute. She caught me staring at her, and the corners of her mouth crimped up.

"We'll talk later, okay?" Dad said, looking at Carla. I looked down. Carla didn't say anything and went inside. I went around the truck and tossed the bat in the back, then opened the door and climbed into the jump seat. Michael was leaning his head against the window, eyes closed. Against his face, my shirt, dark red with scraps of white. My stomach grabbed again. Then, for some reason, I reached over and touched Michael's cheek. "Stop it, asshole," he croaked.

"You should've caught the ball," I whispered, grabbed my hand back. Blood smudged my fingers. My head felt watery, like when I stood on stacked railroad ties looking through Lisa Soto's bathroom window.

Dad started the truck and we left. He flicked on the dome light and unfolded a city map over the steering wheel. "I don't know what to tell your mother about this," Dad said after a while. "You know how she is." He looked at me in the rearview, like he needed a favor. I thought of Mom's on-the-brink voice, her head shaking so much at communion she spilled the wine. I wouldn't tell her, I decided. About me, about Dad, nothing. He was building a house.

My dad one time split open a drunk's head in the Taco Bell parking lot. It was late. We were coming home from a movie. A Suburban swerved into our lane and almost hit us. "Son-ofabitch could've flipped us over the median," Dad said, the veins on his neck standing out. The Suburban went on swerving ahead of us. Mom said let him go, Darnell, he's drunk. But Dad went after him. He wheeled our car into the Taco Bell parking lot right behind the Suburban and got out. Mom started to open her door, but Dad yelled get back in the car, Kay. Michael and me sat in the back, looking out, not knowing what to do. The wind rolled styrofoam cups around the parking lot. In the Taco Bell, some skinny-ass kid, a little older than me, windexed the glass. The drunk scissor-legged it toward the building. When Dad met him at the door, I remember thinking Dad was maybe going to talk to him because he put a hand to the drunk's shoulder, soft, like a tap. The drunk's hands were jammed in his pockets. He turned around, said something to Dad, then grabbed for the door handle. Dad swung and hit the man in the belly and his legs crumpled, like Michael's when the baseball hit him. He went down. Dad poked at the drunk's chest. But the drunk was out. His head had hit the curb. He didn't move. Then the ambulance came. When the police got there, they handcuffed Dad and brought him over to our car. I could see the hair above his wrist was clumped together with the man's blood.

"Bless your hearts," Dad said when he saw me and Michael, like just realizing what he'd done. Michael was crying. Across the parking lot, people from the restaurant stood eyeing us. Mom got some paper towels from the trunk and started wiping Dad's arm, her hand shaking. "Honey, it's okay. I'll be all right," Dad said. He kissed Mom on the cheek. "That guy tried to run us over," I told the cop. His blank face saying you don't matter, go home. The cop said something to Mom in a low voice. Then he took Dad and lowered him into the cop car, protecting his head like they do on TV.

The bloody paper towels in Mom's hand didn't make sense: we were coming home from the movies.

My girlfriend Caroline was on her period the first time we did it. We put an old towel down on her Mom's king-size, but blood soaked right through. In the bathroom mirror, my belly and dick, smeared red. How can you lose so much blood and still be alive? We stripped the sheets off. In the middle of the mattress, surrounding Caroline's wide, dark stain, her mom's faint ones. Rusty countries on a map. Caroline had a dark, muddy smell like the slow spots in the river where duckweed grows. Along the banks once, me and Jeff, minnow-baiting hooks, found a left-behind tackle box and a magazine called *Swizzle Stick*. Women feeling themselves with their fingers. Jesus Fucking Christ, Jeff said, both of us missing something we'd never had. A tight, sad pulling inside. The summer before, someone had hooked a drowned boy's shorts in the duckweed, reeled a cottage-cheese thigh to the top. Divers pulled him out later. He'd gotten caught in the eddy upstream the week before, they guessed. On the bank, me and Jeff smoked weed and talked about catching fish that had nibbled the drowned boy. We'd be cannibals eating them, I said. Jeff saying, Soylent green is people, like Charlton Heston in the movie. Mosquitoes whined in our ears. Our legs and arms red-smudged with their swatted bodies.

One time, my head on Caroline's belly, I imagined being her kid, Dad and Mom erased, like Caroline's black-markered pictures of people who didn't count in our high school yearbook. This is a sick thing I can't tell anyone.

"Your dad's going to move out for a while," Mom told me and Michael at the table the first time Dad left. She stood at the stove holding up a spatula like a microphone. In the electric skillet, our salmon croquettes made spitting sounds. "We have different ideas about some things and we need to sort them out," she said, staring ahead, like she was talking to the spice rack. When she looked at us, her head started shaking. Then she tried to hide it by opening the fridge, bending her head inside and pushing jars around with her hand. I looked at Michael. He stared at his comic book. Mom came over and put the Thousand Island on the table. She turned on the TV and Alex Trebek looked out at us.

Mom sat down at the table. "I'm selling the house," she said, all of a sudden, like touching the TV knob had made a change.

"No shit?" I said. Michael looked up.

"Don't you think we should?" she asked, not hearing my cussing. She looked at me. She forked her salad, waited for me to say something.

"Why?" I said.

"Your dad's going to build us a new one after things settle down," she said.

I bit a huge chunk out of my roll. On the TV, Alex Trebek went over categories.

"I like the way new houses smell," Michael said, filling our gaps.

Mom looked up from her plate. "We forgot to say grace," she said and reached for our hands across the table. Mine was holding a fork but she held it anyway. She said grace with her eyes closed.

Afterwards, we were quiet. On the TV, a contestant said, "What are rhymed couplets?"

Mom didn't say any more about selling the house, only asked us if we liked the food and we nodded, never emptying our mouths, always chewing.

Mom taught English at the community college. Student essays were piled on her desk in the den. Mom called the students her other babies. Freaks, we said. Turban Heads. Jasbeer Mowat was one. "You want mo wat?" Michael kept saying until Mom got mad. "These folks haven't been given everything like you two," she snapped. Once in a while she would read a good one to us. A fifty-year-old woman wrote about going to the doctor for some tests and finding out she had a tumor the size of a cantaloupe in her uterus. Afterwards, the woman went home and prepared her husband and kids for the worst. But when she went back for more tests, they found out the tumor was a baby instead. "What kind of idiot doesn't know they're pregnant?" I'd said. She'd tossed the essay down, glared at me, said I missed the point and besides, what did I know, had I ever been pregnant?

But the best essay, I snagged. I stashed it in the air vent beside my bed. Took some shitty ones too, so it wouldn't look suspicious. Mom pulled her hair out looking for them.

When I got back from smoking weed and watching Letterman at Jeff's, I headed straight up to my room. I grabbed the essay from the vent. Held it under my lamp, its edges brown-smudged from my fingers.

Videsh Deshmuke   Personal Narrative
English 1310   Prof. Kay Greer

DELTA CRASH

My wife Madya and I were returning from my Father's burial ceremony in India. On the plane, I was thinking of how the last meal I prepared for my father—Emperor's Saffron Chicken—was not up to his standards. "A little dry for me," the old bastard said. "And the chutney too lemony." To think how this bothered me then. I wanted so badly to make up to the dead.

On the plane, I remember my wife's head turned toward the window. She was suffering from homesickness already. Her short, modern hair and capped teeth made everyone in my family look a second time. Is this you after all, Madya? their glances said. She did not fit anymore. And because of this, we grieved together. I for my father, her for her old life. It was not that she hated our new life, the life of the Indian restaurant we ran together. It was that she could never taste the other life in the same way.

The night after my father's burial, I lay on the bed in the dark, weeping. She came and sat beside me and ran her fingernails through my hair for a very long time. She sang a song to me in Hindi. Her skin smelled of tea leaves.

On our flight back to Dallas, I remember the many swimming pools below, winking in the sun. Then the plane dropped beneath us, too sudden. Madya grabbed my hand. The oxygen masks fell from the ceiling. There was an explosion. Blue flame rolled down the aisle, like some child's enormous lost ball. Then the world was torn in two.

I was strapped in my seat, sitting in a great field. Sirens were screaming. In my nose, the odor of fuel and something I could not name. Clothing was scattered on the ground. Above, I saw blue sky, darkness, blue sky again. Smoke was coming from a dark, crushed shape in the distance. I felt its heat. I knew the shape was part of our plane. Impossible thoughts whirled in my head. I was outside what a moment before I had been inside. My eyes closed. I still felt Madya's hand in mine. Then I saw my father across the field, hobbling on his bad ankles. He was wearing his white chef's smock and hat. He came to me. "You are certainly lucky," he said in Hindi, patting my shoulder. "A big bird crashes like that and you end up sitting here as though you were watching a movie."

"Father, is Madya still holding my hand?" I asked. He did not answer. He then told me a story. One evening he was cooking at the restaurant and stepped into the dining room. He saw the customers eating his chicken kabobs and curried lamb. He felt satisfied. Then it occurred to him that, just as he had prepared their food, they, in turn, were being prepared for God's terrible appetite. That one day God would lift them up, eat them like nan.

"Is Madya holding my hand?" I asked again.

"We worry over each other, the living and the dead," my father said, looking thoughtful.

"It is not enough. I need her hand," I said.

My father shook his head and told me I was still angry over his criticism of my Emperor's Saffron Chicken.

I remember a baby crying in the distance. At some point, my father hobbled away, and the paramedics found me in the smoke. And, of course, they found Madya's body soon after, in another part of the field.

A half-year ago, a newspaper reporter came by the restaurant. He ordered tandoori-style shrimp. He asked me how my life had changed since the time of the crash, seven years ago. Had I come to terms with my loss? I thought about this. I watched him eat. I remembered Madya running her fingernails through my hair that time, our joined grief. "I am always coming to terms," I said, finally. "It does not end."

My head hummed. I put the essay down, and, for a minute, I saw Videsh in the smoky field with his dad. What they were talking about was important. But I couldn't hear what they were saying because that baby was crying so loud. Then I wondered if Videsh and Madya had a kid somewhere. I thought how babies, before they're born, can hear their parents' voices outside. But words don't go with anything in that dark.

I got up, put the essay back. I turned off the lamp and lay down. Outside, the sprinkler system turned on. Chit, Chit, Chit, it said.

Me and my friend Jeff sat in the storm drain tunnel with our flashlights off. The cement was gritty and cold. Water trickled underneath us. Jeff lit a joint with his lighter, took a hit. Bright speck of heat. We had ditched my brother at the last turn. He didn't have a flashlight. I could hear him yelling my name. Then I heard him say, you motherfucker.

Sounded funny, at first, hearing him frustrated, scared. Jeff was bumping me with his shoulder, squealing into his hand. Then, after a few minutes, Michael's yelling got softer and I could tell he was headed away from us. He sounded old. All of a sudden what we'd done seemed sad and unforgivable, like last winter when Dad put Riley, our dachshund, in the garbage instead of burying her, saying the ground was too frozen.

I could see the outline of Jeff's hand holding the joint. I grabbed it from him and took a hit. My throat burned. "I should go get him," I said. "He'll shit his pants."

"Fuck no," Jeff said. "Let him crawl around awhile. He'll find his way out."

I heard Michael's voice yell my name again from some cold world. I licked my fingers and pinched the joint out. Listening to the water trickling through the pipes, I thought about this tunnel filled up with rain, us trapped inside. I tried to imagine what it would be like being dead, not feeling anything, nobody.

"Listen to that pussy bawl," Jeff said.

I thought for a second about setting Jeff's clothes on fire with the lighter fluid I'd brought in my backpack. Then, on all fours, we headed farther into the tunnel.

In the hospital waiting room, Michael kept saying stupid shit, like how much he missed Riley. Could we get another dog? he wanted to know. A nurse had given him a big wad of gauze to hold on his nose, which had swelled up, huge. His eyes were shiny. Spooky.

Other victims were there. Across from us, a guy in a neck brace stared straight ahead. A Mexican woman with her broken-arm son who the nurses came and got first. He yelped all the way down the hall to the double doors. We watched a Rangers ballgame on the corner-of-the-room TV. After a while, the nurses came for Michael.

"Sugar, you've got to be freezing," the nurse behind the desk said to me, and I remembered I didn't have a shirt on. She brought me a green smock, like doctors wear. "Thanks," I said and pulled it on.

By then, Dad was talking to Mom on the waiting room phone. I heard scraps of it: "Kay, there's no reason to . . . his nose is probably broke, sure, but . . . going to be fine." Dad rubbed his eyes, sighed a few times. Pretty soon Mom would know he wasn't back.

In her chest of drawers, Mom kept envelopes full of our baby teeth. Our first cut hair. Souvenirs of us as kids. But souvenirs of herself too, of who she'd been and wouldn't ever go back to being. My grandma never found a place for my granddad's ashes for the same reason, I think. She gave me his electric shaver. The first time I opened it up, gray beard dust fell out. One night, when Jeff was over, I got it down from the bathroom cabinet. I tapped some of the gray dust into a joint I was rolling and we smoked it in the garage. Afterward, my head all watery, I wondered if there was something wrong with me.

This was why me and Jeff stole stuff, I figured. We hated being stuck as us. Sometimes we'd break into a house, and if older kids lived there, we'd go through their closets, find clothes we could wear. A nice-ass wool overcoat or pair of Doc Martens. And if we found a leftover meal in the fridge, we'd scarf it down. Have Rocky Road ice cream for dessert.

When Dad went in to check on Michael, I decided to wander around the hospital. I walked down the hall to a hospital elevator and got in. It went up and stopped on the second floor, and a candy striper got on with a cart full of flowers. In my nose, a honey smell, thick—like tasting it. The candy striper had a round, pretty face and was big-hipped like Caroline. The sad pulling started on my insides. I wanted Caroline now. I wanted to touch her. The candy striper gave me a shitty look and I stared at the numbers. The elevator stopped on 5.

"You work on this floor?" I asked.

"Yeah. How about you?" she said, sarcastic.

I tugged at my hospital smock. "They gave me this in the emergency room because mine got blood all over it." The door opened and she rolled her cart into the hall. I followed her.

"You save somebody's life or something?" she asked, round-eyed, being funny.

We were in the maternity wing. A sign that said "It's A Boy" hung from a room door. Up ahead, I saw the rows of windows where they bring the newborns.

"No. I hurt my brother," I said.

She looked at me. "On purpose?"

"I don't know," I said. I wanted to tell her more, but she gave me a look that said, "You are not right" and pushed the flower cart faster, past me. Then her big hips disappeared around the corner.

I stopped in front of the baby windows. I could hear their red-faced crying, but it sounded soft on this side of the glass, a tiny whining in your ears. Familiar, too. Like it had always been there but you hadn't noticed. That man, Videsh, heard it, holding his wife's hand in the field. His dad coming back. *We worry over each other, the living and the dead.*

A nurse tapped on the glass. She held a baby up to the window. For a second, I thought she meant me, but then I knew she'd gotten me mixed up with somebody else. She waved his shriveled-up hand at me and I waved back. The baby's feet were smudged black with footprint ink. He looked out, not seeing, not even wondering yet where his dad was, or who would worry over him

Prodigal Fathers

On the phone Kay said, "Where's your integrity, Darnell?" in a voice that threw up its hands. I wasn't sure. I'd just lied about rain pushing back the shooting schedule so I could spend Christmas in Austin with Jo, a woman I'd met working on the movie set three months ago.

"We're slaves to the elements around here," I told Kay on the phone. Around Jo's kitchen window, a string of red pepper lights blinked. The kitchen smelled like oranges and sausage.

"Slaves to something," Kay snapped. She breathed hard into the phone. I sipped my champagne and orange juice and looked across the kitchen at Jo, leaning back against the counter, eating a breakfast taco. She was wearing a pair of too-big train conductor's overalls I'd stolen from wardrobe. White skin shone underneath. Her rusty hair was pinned up and loose strands hung in her face. She dipped her chin and gave me a look like she was staring over an imaginary pair of glasses. Choose, the look said.

Jo sometimes sang open mike night at the Hobbyhorse, a bar off Highway 290, near the state park where we were shooting. Old country standards. Patsy Cline. Kitty Wells. From the stage, her voice wavered, dipped, rose. *I've been so wrong for so long.* On those nights, a hum started somewhere under my ribs and spread downward. But I worried that if I stared too long, it would fade, the way a dream does in the shower. So I'd drunk beer and watched the orchid pattern of her dress out of the corner of my eye.

Kay knew about Jo, though not the specifics. When I was home two months ago, Kay and I got drunk at dinner on a few bottles of merlot and played Scrabble with our Prozac-repaired friend, Bill Comeaux. We'd met Bill in grief counseling. "Oh that's choice. You correcting *me*," Kay said when I challenged FEALTY and won—she'd spelled it with an I. Kay scattered plastic letters onto the floor. "Fealty's wasted on people like you," she said, glaring. Bill sipped his wine and shot me a nervous smile. I winked, told Bill he'd have to do the challenging next time. That same night, after Bill left, I drunkenly suggested Kay might be happier if she found a boyfriend. It would be okay with me, I told her, since we couldn't seem to comfort one another. I felt my stomach flutter when I said it. Then I didn't feel anything and it didn't seem like the truth at all, only a jumble of words. "What?" Kay said from the doorway. "What?" She was squinting like she was underwater and couldn't make out the blur in front of her. "Go fuck yourself, Darnell," she said in a voice like a bedsheet ripping. I wondered if I already had. She tinkered with her shelf full of Japanese tea sets, their tiny orbiting cups. Then she stared at me, clear-eyed. "Why did you stop building houses?" she asked as if she'd peeled back rough skin and found the heart of our trouble. I tried to think of a reasonable answer. "I never liked the people who lived in them," I said, finally, certain it was true. I wandered into the living room and popped my tape of *Red River* into the VCR, exactly where I'd left off the night before. On the screen, Joanne Dru fretted over Montgomery Clift. Down the hall, I heard Kay shut our sons' bedroom doors, though one was sleeping at a friend's and the other was, of course, dead.

On the phone in Jo's kitchen, I told Kay I'd be home three days after Christmas. I'd drive our son Michael out to Waxahachie to hunt down a tree, like Dad and I used to. Sure, it wouldn't be Christmas day, but we'd make the most of it, I said. My voice sounded strange, a mix of assurance and panic. Thoughts stuttered. I felt like a bad actor, like I'd been cast but couldn't carry off the part. "We can decorate it together," I told her, quiet, the receiver close to my mouth. Out of the corner of my eye, I could see Jo holding a bottle of champagne. I turned to her for—what? consolation?—but she'd grabbed my glass off the table and was refilling it. Her face was tight. She was standing still, staring at the bubbles, like she was conducting an important experiment. I wanted to hang up, but I wanted to give Kay hope, too.

"Well aren't you Mr. Traditional," Kay said in a limp voice. In the background, Elvis sang "Silent Night."

"I get it from my dad," I told her, letting her sarcasm roll right off. I'm not cynical. For the most part, I think we do the best we can, with uneven results. Dad used to take me to a Christmas tree farm every year to cut our own tree. One year, when I was about eight, we hit and killed a buck with our car on the way. When Dad and I got out to look, the buck was lying on its side and one of its legs was still kicking. Each kick seemed measured and natural, not jerky like you'd expect. It seemed he would've been there kicking the cold air even without our help. Then he stopped. Dad walked to the car and fiddled with a cracked headlight. I could see tufts of brown hair stuck in the car's grill, specks of blood. Later, when we came back with our Christmas tree, we passed a man strapping the dead deer to the top of his station wagon. "Two trophies in one day," Dad joked. "He's lucky we were so generous."

My recent good fortune: Jo's ex-husband wanted to hurt me, though he didn't know how badly yet. He was young. It takes time to sort out which feelings go with which actions. The fire he set in my truck was a start. And, though I knew I'd never use it, I kept a gun under my charred truck seat as a deterrent. My dad was a safety engineer for an oil company and stowed this same .38 in an Imperial cigar box when he traveled around. When I was little, he used to joke that if he met any trouble, he'd hand out cigars.

On the phone, Kay wasn't saying anything. Along Jo's windowsill sat sunlight-spattered Mexican knickknacks she'd picked up from Ciudad Acuña. In a yellow-painted clay helicopter, half a dozen grinning skeletons rose to heaven. The pilot leered out of the cockpit as if he knew something they didn't.

In 1977, Dad was burned up in a refinery fire just outside Fordyce, Arkansas. They found his ashes stretched alongside those of the office cat, Harold. All together, Dad and Harold weighed less than a can of coffee. Against my advice, Mother keeps the urn in her china cabinet, and, beside it, champagne glasses etched with their wedding date. Setting the table or doing a crossword, she can glance up at him, at least I know where he is, she thinks. I've considered grabbing the urn some Christmas while she's out visiting her sister, tossing his ashes into the Ouachita River, which eventually joins the Mississippi somewhere near Baton Rouge, Louisiana. From there, it's out to sea.

"Maybe we won't be here," Kay said on the phone, cracking the silence.

"What's that mean?" I asked, the miscast feeling returning.

"I guess I don't know. I just want everything to quit happening."

The thought that Kay had taken my wayward advice about the boyfriend suddenly blindsided me. I pictured Bill Comeaux and Kay cooking dinner. Wineglasses on the counter. Bill's shaky, side-effect hands seizing her shoulders, a moment of passion. Kay, still holding a whisk, stabbing at a mixing bowl. They'd collapse to the floor, sobbing.

On the phone, Kay didn't say anything for a few seconds, then she asked, if I had time when I got back, could I mount the basketball goal she'd gotten as a Christmas present for Michael? Sure, I said. Then she hung up.

Jo pulled a zip-lock baggie from the freezer, came over, and sat down at the table. She unzipped the baggie and took out what looked like a shriveled gold tongue and laid it in front of me. It was a used condom. Splinters of frost clung to its tip. Jo stroked my arm with her smooth, small-boned hand. For a few seconds we just sat there in the quiet, a wedge of sun flaring off the table.

I drank my champagne and orange juice down. I poked the condom with my finger. I stared at it stupidly.

"Preserves," Jo said, narrowing her eyes at me. She spun the condom on the table with her finger.

"Whose?" I asked.

Jo said, "What do you care? It's my Christmas present to myself."

"You're keeping a man's semen in your freezer. I think I'm entitled to know whose it is." My face felt numb.

"Entitled? Why?"

"I sleep with you," I said.

"So did this fella," Jo said.

"It's kind of sick, don't you think?"

"If it was yours, would you feel that way?"

"Is it mine?" I said, feeling suddenly hopeful.

"No."

My stomach fell.

Jo climbed onto my lap. She pressed her breasts against me. She cupped the back of my head and kissed my mouth. Hair strands caught in my teeth. She pulled away. "It's a secret," she said. "I stuck it in a hotel ice bucket when the donor fell asleep." She smiled, the tip of her tongue between her teeth. "Brilliant, huh?" She let go of my head. Her face stiffened, serious. "Darnell, I'm thirty-four. I've miscarried twice. If you won't knock me up, he will." She tapped the condom with a fingernail.

I pictured Jo, her tiny, black-stockinged feet shuffling over a white marble hotel lobby, an ice bucket under one arm. I knew it was more scientific than that. But I believed her, sitting in that kitchen. She had a biology degree. Before working for Parks and Wildlife, she'd worked on a catfish farm raising channel cats from eggs. Preserves. It seemed possible.

Even though I was hundreds of miles from the town I'd always lived in, severed from my other, paler life with Kay and Michael, it still seemed possible I might retrace my steps and reenter that life, take Michael camping at Lake Whitney or help Kay retile the guest bathroom.

"Darnell, you know what the H. stands for in Jesus H. Christ?" Jo asked, tossing her hair from her face. "Haploid." She laughed.

"Haploid?" I stared, confused.

"Jesus doesn't have a human father, see, so he's only got one set of chromosomes. Essentially he fertilized himself."

On the table, I could see the condom glistening.

On Christmas Eve, Jo and I went to the Hobbyhorse Bar. Some of the movie people were there, hunched over beers. Production people, set designers, a few stranded actors. Merle Haggard sang "Ramblin' Fever" over the speakers.

Upright against the bar leaned the canvas-wrapped body of *Lonesome Dove*'s Gus McCrae someone had bought at a prop auction. A Santa hat perched on its head. Gerry Hutka, one of the assistant producers, patted the body on the back. "You think Gus here gets paid union scale?" Gerry asked. He got two mugs from the bartender and poured us margaritas from his pitcher. Gerry was fifty-two. His face was puffy and red from allergies. A few months earlier, Gerry's asthma had flared up so bad, his heart went crazy. The doctors thought he was about to have a cardiac arrest so they induced a kind of coma. During this coma, Gerry had a vision that wires were sticking out of his chest. People he cared about held onto them. His wife and brother were there. He said he knew if he cut those wires, or if the people let go, he'd die. But they held on. He made it through. Later, in a *National Geographic,* he found a picture of some Hindu men with hooks piercing the skin of their backs and attached to these hooks were taut ropes held by other men. "It was like that," he told us, showing us the glossy clipping. "I could feel them tugging."

In the bar Gerry kissed Jo on the cheek and said, "Guess who poured me a Mexican martini last night?" He waited. "Lee Harvey Oswald's daughter. Swear to God."

"Where?" I said.

"At the Chili Parlor. A guy at the bar told me she waitresses there. Sure enough, the door opens, and I see a woman with sandy-brown hair, putting her purse behind the bar. She's late twenties. Pretty in an angular way. All elbows and collarbone. Same dark eyes, I noticed right off. Well, there's lots of Texas memorabilia on the walls in there. And for some reason, who the fuck knows why, above one of the tables, someone's hung a framed newspaper photo of Jack Ruby shooting Lee Harvey Oswald. The guy at the bar said it's been there since the seventies. Lee Harvey, his eyes closed, mouth gaping, like he might be belting out words to a song. The guy says she was born right before he was shot, so she never really met him. All she knows are photos. Nearly every night, she has to smile and carry sweaty beers to that table, a photo of her dead father right above it." Gerry drank from his mug.

"Why does she work there then?" I asked.

"Well, why don't they just take the picture down?" Jo said, stiffening up.

"The guy said she doesn't want anyone to know, so she keeps quiet," Gerry said, ignoring my question. "She needs the job." Gerry fingered his lime wedge. "I've seen that image, I guess, a hundred times. It never meant anything to me. A famous man, getting shot. That's all. I didn't know him. But at first, sitting at the bar, I couldn't look her in the eye."

Jo propped her elbows on the table, rested her chin in her hands. "You felt bad? Like ashamed?"

"Maybe. I guess so. I felt like I'd cheated or something. Like I'd peeked in her window."

"You sure you didn't?" I asked.

"What?" Gerry said, like I'd spoken a language he couldn't understand. He was drunk. His eyes were jittering around. I looked at Jo. She was twisting a straw between her fingers. I wanted Gerry to shut up.

"Finally, I asked her what her name was," Gerry said, "even though I already knew it. Rachel. We talked for a while. I told her I worked in the movies. You know what her favorite Western is? *Stagecoach*." Gerry looked over at Jo. "John Wayne's the Cisco Kid. Claire Trevor's the whore with a heart of gold. Great flick." He smiled and eased back in his chair. "Later on, I thought about asking her out for some coffee." For a second, Gerry didn't say anything. Then he said, "But it wasn't like I wanted to get in her pants."

"Right," I said, grinning. Jo shot me a look.

Gerry sipped his margarita. "I didn't ask her out, though. Around closing, her boyfriend, or whoever, showed up and that was that."

"We ought to toast something," I said, raising my mug.

"To those who can't be with us," Gerry said in a wobbly, mock-drunk voice. We toasted and he looked right at me, smiling. Then the smile faded and he looked over at another table. I knew he was thinking about my son Andrew. I wanted to tell him it was okay, that a toast was nothing but cheap sentiment anyway, like his Rachel story.

Jo was looking out the window at the dark. She seemed gloomy and far away. I tried to think of a way to cheer her up. "Let's go look at Christmas lights," I said, finally.

We left Gerry at the bar, climbed in Jo's Buick and headed down Guadalupe Street until we hit 37th, where strings of colored lights stretched over the street. Roofs and porches hung thick with them, like cobwebs. Flaming tiki torches lined one front yard.

We parked and walked up the street. It had gotten colder and the wind was blowing. We downed our beers and I stuck the bottles in someone's trash. A man with a sleeping child in a backpack passed us. A few bundled couples walked up ahead. Blinking red and gold lights curlicued through the trees.

Under the glare, Jo's features were thrown into relief. Her eyes deepened. I imagined her as a mother with worry lines, then an old woman, a silver braid of hair. She saw me looking at her. "Stop it, you," she said, her forehead wrinkling. A mother's scold, I thought, feeling the familiar hum under my ribs. "I'm a lucky man," I said, and felt this was mostly true. I pictured our future daughter waddling through our own light-drenched yard. I would bring her Mexican sweet breads from Del Rio, where we were filming some border saga. I'd come home to her mother's warm breast.

"I don't think so," Jo said.

"What?"

"That you're a lucky man."

I reached for her hand, but she walked ahead.

In one yard, a small TV was suspended from an oak branch by wires. Its pale glow flickered over the yard. Jo and I walked into the grass where a couple was standing, watching. On the screen, the Grinch's piled-high sleigh teetered on a mountaintop.

"Christ, I need to pee," I whispered to Jo. I looked down the nearly empty street. When the TV-watching couple left, I slunk off down the side of the house. At the back of their property, it was dark and trees were clumped together. All the light from the street seemed soaked up. Unzipping, I could see a woman and little boy framed in the sliding glass door playing some kind of board game on the coffee table.

Standing there holding my penis, I imagined catastrophe: What if they saw me? Flashlights. Howling dogs. What would they think when they brought me into the light?

Ron, Jo's ex, called us up about one A.M. "Merry Christmas, cocksucker," he said.

"Ron, you can get arrested for phone harassment," I said, calm, though my heart hammered. I didn't know if you could get arrested or not, but I figured Ron didn't know either. "I didn't press charges for the fire. That was a gift."

Click.

"My ex?" Jo asked in a sleepy voice.

"Whenever he calls to apologize, somehow threats slip out," I said.

To drive Ron off, Jo had told him about my stay in the Travis County jail on assault charges, but left out the details. A drunk fell down outside a bar and claimed I shoved him. Not the stuff you'd tell your kids about, but hardly intimidating. In jail, they give you square oranges with your lunch. No one could tell me how they got that way. A minor wonder. They come in a paper bag along with a peanut butter or egg salad sandwich.

After Ron's call, I couldn't sleep. I went into Jo's living room, found my tape of *Rio Grande*, with John Wayne and Maureen O'Hara. Wayne's a cavalry officer holding off the Apaches. He and Maureen O'Hara haven't seen each other for sixteen years. They have a son who's enlisted in Wayne's regiment. She comes out to force her husband's hand, so to speak. He's supposed to choose, the Apache or his family. Miraculously, he gets both.

"All that dirt's sinking in on him," Kay said when it started to rain the afternoon we buried Andrew. We were in her sister Maggie's dining room, linen on the table, our plates covered with untouched food. Aunts and uncles doddered up for dessert and coffee.

Roller skates on wood. That's what the thunder sounded like.

When Kay started shrieking, Maggie and my Aunt Jessie led her back to the bedroom. I walked with her halfway, still carrying a buttered roll in one hand. I put my other hand to her shoulder. She snatched it off without looking at me. "Kay didn't know what she was doing, Darnell," my Aunt Jessie said later. "Sure," I said.

When I was little, my Aunt Jessie told me to say knock wood and rap my knuckles on whatever was handy, wood or not, so I wouldn't jinx my luck.

When the two cops knocked on the door, I thought it was about my unpaid speeding tickets. Once, back when I built houses, I'd seen my tape and float man handcuffed on the job and taken off to jail. So I hid in the utility room. Kay answered the door. They came inside and I could hear low voices in the living room. But then the washer changed cycles and I couldn't hear anything. I cracked the door. On the couch, I saw the backs of their heads. Kay raked through her cropped hair with her fingers, a nervous gesture from years ago when it hung down to her rear. When they got up to come get me, the spin cycle was going. Kay flicked on the light and I froze. Her face seemed bruised in the harsh light. Her eyes were red. "Hey there," I said in a bold voice, my eyes jumping from her, to the cops, to a shirt I was holding and beginning to fold. And then they told me Andrew had been shot.

Andrew and his buddy Jeff had broken into a house. It was afternoon. No one was supposed to be home. They'd pried open a back window using a metal file from my toolbox. They'd done this before. Inside, they tracked mud across the salt-and-pepper Berber carpet, found a bottle of vodka, drank some of it with Tang and finished the leftover pizza in the fridge. At some point, Andrew spilled his drink on his new down jacket. Then they somehow found time to un-plug the stereo, VCR, and bread maker and stack them in the entryway. Andrew sauntered off to the bedroom for more. The door was closed. The man who lived there was sick with the flu, the cops said. Someone from his work had driven him home. He was sleeping and heard a racket in the kitchen.

The shotgun blast ripped away most of Andrew's jaw.

Down stuffing floats in the empty doorway. Fade out. That's how it would be in a movie.

• • •

In the hospital, they rigged a covering for the missing half of Andrew's jaw. Before they did it, I saw the length of his tongue inside there. Saw where it connected to bone in back, its obscene purple beginnings. I couldn't take my eyes off it. Once, when the nurse left the room, I felt at the back of my own tongue with my fingers and gagged.

They put in a tube to relieve the pressure on his brain. Fifty–fifty, they said. First twenty-four hours critical.

Michael wouldn't go in. He played his Game Boy in the waiting room.

When we called relatives about Andrew, we didn't give details. There had been an accident, we said.

In the hospital room, the machines whirred and beeped. Kay and I held Andrew's hand. We loved and forgave each other with fervor and hope.

He lived three days.

"False hope is a prick tease," Jo told me the morning I left to have a belated Christmas with Kay and Michael. She was in the kitchen repotting some rosemary. Her fingers were black with dirt. "You make promises you can't deliver, Darnell."

"I'm following through," I said.

"Part of you is," she said, "but the other part's cut away."

I winced. Felt around with my hand, found my crotch. "Which part, you think?"

I carried an armload of Christmas presents outside, piled them in my truck seat and headed for Ft. Worth.

• • •

I pulled in front of my split-level in the early afternoon. Bare
tree limbs and power lines broke up the sky. In the yard, Kay
had made some changes. A birdhouse swayed on a pole
wound with blinking Christmas lights. Flat stones the size of
garbage can lids made a path to the front steps. I wondered
if Michael had helped her with these projects.

Inside the house, Christmas presents were piled in a
corner of the living room, waiting for the tree. Kay had
moved the furniture, bought a new rug and a lamp. A coffee
table with inlaid tile my father made was gone, but I pretended not to notice. "The place looks great," I said, hugging
Kay. She smelled like maple syrup and lemon peel. I pulled
her to me lightly, not sure what was required. She kissed me
on the cheek, smiled, and pulled away. "You look nice too,"
I said. And she did. She had on a new dark green dress and
white hose. She'd let her hair grow out.

"Thanks. I'm experimenting a little," she said, touching
her hair. She stared at something on my shoulder, then with
her hand, brushed it away. "Flour," she said. "I've been
baking." She folded her arms in front of her. "So, how's the
soggy cowboy epic coming?"

"Swimmingly," I said.

"Ha. Ha." Kay grinned in spite of herself. "You and
Michael should have fun on the tree hunt—your sophisti-
cated senses of humor."

We stood there in the living room for a little while, not
saying anything. "Would you like some wine?" she asked. I
thought about what I'd said about a boyfriend last time and
hesitated. "A glass with lunch, sure," I said. Kay went

through the kitchen door and it swung closed behind her. In the dining room, I could see the table was set, candles burning. I could hear the TV down the hall, where Michael was. From the kitchen, glasses clinked, then the oven whumped closed. Kay's feet crossed the wood floor. A cabinet door slapped shut.

I knew a movie sound engineer who used dozens of microphones to record the sounds of his house so he could dub them into movies later. Kitchen door creak, take one. Water groan in pipes, take two. Private sounds of his very own life. "Even after I'm dead," he said, "I'll still be making noise."

Standing there in my living room, it struck me that I had no private sounds, nothing to save.

I wandered down the hall and found Michael in the den watching TV. "Howdy do," I said, waving from the doorway. "I made it. Ready to get that tree?"

It was nearly dark when Michael and I drove back from Waxahachie with the tree. Beside the road, the fields were great stretches of purple. A lit billboard offered tracts of land at bargain prices. Another said LIVE THE WAXAHACHIE WAY but didn't give instructions. Every once in a while, the wind gusted and I could hear the tree shift on the camper top.

Michael fiddled with the radio, then turned it off. "I'd hate to live out in nowhere like this," he said.

"Now you think that way, but later you wouldn't mind it so much," I said. "I'm serious. There are worse places."

"Where?"

"Wichita, Kansas. Cold. Ugly. Gray. Sirens wailing all night. You were a toddler. Andrew was eight."

I wasn't sure why I'd brought this up. Who wanted to hear about worse places? Michael was quiet for a long time. He opened the glove box and got a U.S. road atlas out and thumbed through it. I wanted to lift the dusky silence off us. "Andrew was a crazy little kid," I said, looking over at him. No reaction. "He set his bed on fire, once." Wind whistled around the window. "Andrew took your granddad's Zippo from my chest of drawers and crawled under his bed to test it. The darkest place he could find, he said later. Well, the gauzy stuff under the box springs caught fire. Andrew ran out of the house screaming. I ran to his room. You couldn't see the ceiling for the smoke. I crawled under the bed with a wet towel and smothered it. The hairs on my forearm singed right off. Anyway, afterwards, we went outside, looked down the street, called him. No Andrew. It was nearly dark. Your mother was worried." I paused.

"Where'd he go?" Michael asked. Concern flickered through his face and was gone.

"A neighbor found him up a high-voltage tower, sitting thirty feet off the ground. He thought he'd burned up the house and us with it. He could see the damage better up there, I guess. He was scared. He wasn't coming down. Fire department pulled him off. They're always there when you need them, right?" I laughed, looked over at Michael. His face was a blank. "See, Andrew thought they were coming to arrest him."

"Yeah," Michael said, like he wasn't listening anymore. He was staring at the purple fields.

"Anyway, later on, he didn't want to go back into his room because of the smell. You guys roomed together for a while."

Scrubby oak trees flew by. As the road dipped, I could see cows' dark bodies along a creek bed. We were thirty minutes away from the house. Kay would have a ham and casseroles ready. Pecan pie. After dinner, we'd decorate the tree, open presents. Maybe watch a movie together.

"I can only stay a few days," I told Michael. "We're doing some filming in Del Rio the next few weeks. You ever want to come out some weekend, just say the word, Bird."

"Do you have a girlfriend in Austin?" Michael looked at me steady, as if it was the most reasonable question he could think to ask.

My stomach rolled.

I pretended to check my side-view mirror. I thought about earlier when I'd stopped off to call Jo at a pay phone and she'd asked about Michael, wondering if he'd liked the rod and reel she'd picked out. I explained we hadn't gotten to the presents yet. Then she said maybe she should call the house later and ask him personally. I laughed, but I was nervous.

"No," I told Michael. "No girlfriend. Does your mom think I have one?"

He shrugged.

I tried to think of something to say, words that would fall meaningfully into place, like in Scrabble. Single truths about relationships, integrity. How you get to remote locations from familiar places. I thought of John Wayne in *Rio Grande*. He gets to know a son he's never seen and falls in love with

Maureen O'Hara all over again. I tried to pair my fatherly urge with a comforting gesture, a pat on Michael's knee or shoulder, but nothing would come.

In my rearview, the car behind me started to pass, but pulled back. Its headlights glared off the mirror.

"I heard a joke," I said. "But don't tell your mom I told you this, okay? You'll get me into trouble."

Michael nodded, rolled his eyes.

"There's a guy on an airplane sitting next to this lady. The guy keeps sneezing. The lady notices after each sneeze he sticks a tissue down the front of his pants and wipes himself. Finally, she can't take any more and asks what the problem is. Another sneeze. Another wipe. 'Well Ma'am,' he says, 'I've got this peculiar medical condition. Every time I sneeze, I have an orgasm.' 'My God,' she says, 'is there anything you take for this?' 'Pepper,' he says." I looked over at Michael, grinned. Michael's face was turned to the window.

Whump. I heard the tree before I saw it in the rearview. For a second, branches hung in the camper window, red-stained by taillights. Ropes whipped the air. Then it fell onto the road. The car behind us swerved hard onto the shoulder. Its lights went sideways, then off into the trees.

"What was that?" Michael looked out the back and then at me. I slowed down. From where we were, I couldn't see them.

I thought about stopping, turning around, seeing if everybody was okay, retrieving the tree. But what if they weren't okay? What if they had whiplash or broken bones? And the worst thing—I wasn't thinking of them. I was thinking I had warrants on unpaid tickets. An expired license. They'd pick me up. Revoke my probation. "I'm not sure, but we could've lost a tree back there," I said.

"Why don't you pull over?" Michael asked, turning around in the seat, looking out the back. "Dad?"

I kept driving. Outside, dark shapes rushed by. I tried to think of what to do. I grabbed my wallet to tuck it under the seat in case we were stopped. On the back of my license it says Organ Donor. I'd never given it much thought until we donated Andrew's kidneys and liver—people walking around with parts of other people inside them. Wouldn't you wonder what the donor was like? Wonder if some of that goodness or badness might rub off inside?

Michael watched me, his face splotchy in the dash glow. He waited for an answer. Loose ropes slapped the camper top. Ahead, in the distance, clusters of lights, neighborhoods. I was headed toward them, but it seemed any moment, I would ease onto the shoulder, turn around, undo what had been done.

One Flesh, One Blood

THEY COULDN'T KNOW I'D LOST PART OF MYSELF BECAUSE they'd never felt a body wrenched from their own, or held a clamoring mouth to their breast. Father Howard saying, Darnell and Michael need you here. But my skin felt raw in the places they touched. I wanted to go into that deep muddy hole with Andrew then. A mortal sin to take your life. But why? So God can go on filling us up and then wrenching away what we give him?

I couldn't take communion for a long time afterwards. With Father Howard, I tried. But when he blessed the wine with his dry-knuckled fingers, my head started shaking. He had touched Andrew. When I was little, my mother warned me about touching the soft spot in my baby sister's skull, about what careless fingers could do. Go right through to their brain.

During Mass, I had to cross myself and leave.

• • •

My friend Aileen drove in the day after the funeral. Eight months pregnant, her face rounded, but underneath, the same effortless good looks I resented when we were younger. Her olive skin and small nose. Aileen, back then, flustered by compliments, looking away because she didn't believe the truth. And in photos, my pale skin always washing out like a ghost's. In tenth grade, we both played French horn, each shying from competition with the other, but each, I knew, conjuring the other's failures—a missed open C or weak embouchure. Not enough to humiliate, but enough to link us together in uncertainty. And with boys, I savored her few rejections as compensation for my aloneness. Wanting her to hurt, so I could offer solace. Both of us curled inward like our brass horns.

In my entryway, Aileen's hard belly pressed against mine. Her neck smelled like lavender soap. She'd come a day late because her husband Larry had to drive her from Nashville—her doctor wouldn't let her fly. Larry brought her bags in from the car, said a soft hello to me, and wandered down the hall, looking for the bathroom. Aileen and I didn't talk about anything for some time, just stood, holding. The silence a relief to me because there had been too much talk after the funeral. The clasped hands and hugs. Husks of feeling. Then rain had slapped on the eaves and I'd thought of the shifting mound of dirt over him.

In the kitchen, I poured us each a glass of wine, and Aileen sat with me at the table. I reached over, made furrows in her hair with my fingers, looking for gray. "Look what I found," I said and pretended to pluck one, holding it up. Aileen gave me a weak smile, then leaned forward, the side of her head resting against my breastbone, as if listening for my heart. And then she shook against me and I knew she was crying. I felt a sudden quiver of envy from our earlier lives. Felt the inequity of the child she carried. Then this dissolved, and I only felt ashamed because I couldn't cry.

The summer after tenth grade, Aileen and I lied about our ages to take jobs waiting tables at the Candlelight Inn. We wore starched white shirts that afterwards always smelled of cigar smoke and fried catfish. We swigged left-behind drinks and mostly played at being adult, flirting with tables of college boys. All that summer, Aileen seemed to be shedding her awkwardness, leaving me. Once, after our shift, we drove out to a party with two college boys. On the way, one of the boys poured us whiskey in plastic cups. I sniffed mine. Aileen said "salud," and downed hers. I looked at her. Salud? "That's the way," the boy driving said and laughed, lifting his cup. Then Aileen leaned over the front seat and I watched her head bob and swoop between them as she talked. Watched her improvise familiarity, her hands lightly touching their shoulders. So later, at the party, when she got sick in the backyard hammock, and the boys had to drive us home early, I was glad of it. She lay on the back seat, my hand smoothing her dark bangs.

My father, forty-five then and still handsome, taught senior English at our high school. Diabetes made his feet swell and nearly cost him the toes off his right foot the year before. Sometimes when I had band practice, I'd see him walking gingerly to his car as if the pavement was shattered glass. He wasn't supposed to drink alcohol or eat sweets, but couldn't help himself. At home, he'd wait until my mother was asleep to get his scotch from the garage. My mother would look for chocolate bars, find them hidden under couch cushions, inside loafers. "A gun would be quicker," she'd said to him once, holding up a half-eaten Heath bar. My mother once told me she'd dreamed that she woke up one morning, pulled back the covers and my father's legs were gone. Does he think he's the only one suffering? she'd asked me then in a sharp voice, the dream still holding sway. But she loved him. Most nights, my father would prop his legs on the couch and she'd rub his gray, bloated feet and he'd read to her. But then his face began to sag, and he started going to bed early, without reading. Sometimes, I'd try to head off his humiliation, fumble through his coat pockets and briefcase for the chocolate bars before Mother did, find and eat them in my room.

Touched meant crazy. My sister and I once saw Mrs. Arceneaux talking to herself after church and Mom said, "Poor Harriet is touched," and tapped her own temple.

Coming home from Andrew's baseball practice, I saw that Carla woman's car in front of Darnell's office. This was right

after he told me he was back to stay. Andrew and Michael
were arguing, making breath catch in my chest. I screamed
at them, pulled at my stiff neck. They stared. "Whatever,"
Andrew said. I turned into the Foodland parking lot, and left
them in the still-running car. The sky bled at its edges. Heat
rose off the asphalt. I went inside and wandered down aisles.
The harsh light making everything garish. I didn't want anything, but then I thought how hot it was and saw the watermelons along the floor, like kept promises. My sister and I
finding my father's watermelons floating in our iced bathtub.
I thumped a few with my finger but couldn't tell one from
another. Then I picked one up and cradled it in my arms. I
walked through the express line and out the door. The push
of heat. Exhaust. A train of shopping carts clattered by. My
arms ached. I took quick half-steps toward a dented
Oldsmobile with its windows down. I pushed the water-
melon through the back window, opened the passenger door
and got in. Taped along the sun visor was a yellowed picture
of a little sandy-blonde girl with her overweight mother.
There were smells of another life in there. Sweat. Corn chips.
Sunscreen. And behind these, a dry sweetness like dead
flowers. On the floor, blue pamphlets were scattered that said
Jehovah's Witnesses on the front. I looked out over the
parking lot. My car a row over, my sons' heads inside. The
distance between us.

Once, after coming home drunk from a party, I saw my father through the porch window, reading at his desk. This was

before he became so depressed, before the sharp angles of his face dulled. He was bent over a large book. In one hand he held a glass of scotch—my mother, long asleep, didn't know. Secrets, though they distance us, keep us whole, too. But my mother thought if we didn't confess our sins, they would eat us alive.

My parents met by chance. They both lived in student apartments at the university. One day, a Mexican woman from across the street ran screaming to each apartment, banging on doors. My father and mother, the only ones home in the middle of the day, went with the woman to her house, walked through her living room where the grandmother sat on the couch softly singing, and into the water-slick bathroom where a one-year-old girl lay naked on the floor, her mouth slack. Toys floated in the tub. Mi hija, the woman moaned. They rode with the woman and grandmother to the hospital, though it was already too late. The woman told my father the grandmother was supposed to watch the girl for a few minutes while she put up groceries. But the senile grandmother had forgotten and wandered into the bedroom leaving the child alone in the bathtub. "My mother is half in that other place," the woman said, holding the grandmother's hand, forgiving her. My father told me this made a deep impression on him.

My father found the family a motel room for the week so they didn't have to face that bathroom. A few days later, my mother lit some dinner candles, invited my father over for Hungarian goulash.

On the porch, I fiddled with the key in the lock, giving

my father time to put away his scotch glass. I pushed the door and went inside. My steps around the dining room felt large and dreamlike, like the fairy tale giant with ten-league boots. But when I came into the den, my father didn't seem to notice my clumsiness. He said, "Hey there pumpkin," and took off his glasses, rubbed his eyes. I told him hello, smoothed my skirt and leaned against the wall. He put his glasses back on, looked me over. "Don't you look nice," he said. I said thanks and asked what he was reading.

"A book from the Middle Ages about the grail king." He picked up the book again, held it up so I could see. "The author, Wolfram, was a German poet, but he was a knight too." My father thumbed through the book until he found an underlined passage and read it. "My brother and I are one body—like good man and good wife. One flesh and one blood, here battling from loyalty of heart, and doing itself much harm."

I told him I liked it. His voice in that room made me feel good, its resonance. Then I noticed the scotch glass on the desk beside him and I felt a rightness about it, like we were conspiring against something, and I didn't have to speak in guarded sentences or pretend. We shared our secrets. He asked about my night, and I told him I'd gone to a bar with some friends to listen to a band.

"Did you do any dancing?"

"No. It wasn't the kind of music you dance to," I said.

"Your mother and I used to go dancing out on the Jacksboro Highway." He smiled and looked like he was re-membering some past when his feet glided, smooth and painless, over wood floors, a time when he and my mother slept soundlessly, without bad dreams. "Dancing's the thing," he said. "It'll come back around." He smiled.

We were quiet for a long while, not minding.

Every Thursday Darnell and I would drive up to the church rectory and have potluck with our fellow grievers. That's where we met Bill. He was tall and stooped and whenever he got up from his chair, he'd slap his thighs in a way that made you think he might say something dramatic. But he never did. He was quiet and I suppose that's why Darnell didn't like him.

Bill's wife had been killed in an auto accident the week after our son Andrew was shot. Six months later, he still stared at you in a daze and his face was haggard and bruised looking.

"Are you eating?" I asked Bill, after our group session.

"Some," he said. "A little."

"I'm worried about you," I said.

Darnell came over, patted Bill's shoulder and asked him to dinner, the lines along his forehead bunching in sympathy. You're sincere, not honest. This is what I would tell him later when he decided not to come to these meetings with me anymore because he didn't feel committed. Sincerity is here, then gone, but honesty you have to struggle with.

He would tell me I'm splitting hairs.

• • •

Aileen and I were marrying ketchup bottles at the end of our shift when she told me about my dad. This is how I pictured it:

Aileen was wearing a man's fedora, sitting cross-legged in my father's recliner, holding her Dante essay. The fedora was her totem for our senior year, she'd said. My father stood, hands in pockets, leaning over her shoulder. His feet ached terribly, but he wanted to look authoritative. No one else was home. "Dante's image of Beatrice," my father read from her essay, "led him out of his dark wood." Then, he took his hand from his pocket and seemed about to turn the page, but instead brushed Aileen's right breast. He then leaned over her, crumpled her paper, and kissed her on the mouth.

At the table, Aileen fingered a ketchup cap, not looking at me. "Your dad fell all over himself apologizing and I left. I drove off," she said, her voice wavering. "I've been waiting to tell you." Her fingers felt along her mouth.

I stared at Aileen's milky nails. Then I told her she must have given my father ideas, always touching the way she did.

She didn't talk to me for a month.

Darnell left. One afternoon, six months after Andrew died, we lay on the couch in our living room and he wanted inside me, and I told him I wasn't ready yet, my neck strung tight. His fingers paused on my breasts. The weight of him bearing down on me. I held my breath. This will pass, I thought. Outside, I heard a neighbor's leaf blower start up.

"Am I going too fast?" Darnell asked, a gentle catch to his voice. I touched his face, out of habit, my hand saying, it's not you, but me, my cold raw body. Then I snatched my hand away because he was the reason my son was dead, his helplessness. We lay there in silence. I buttoned my blouse. Then he got up and went outside. Five days later he left.

"Something's happened to your mother," my father said from his hospital bed after the shrieking started. He looked toward the hallway and then at me, glassy-eyed from the Darvon the nurse had given him. An oxygen tube clung to his nose. He tried to pull it out and sit up.

"That's a lady down the hall, Daddy," I said, squeezing his arm, helping him lie back. "Mother went home to get some rest."

Another shriek.

"What are they doing to her?" he asked, his face tightening. After a few seconds it went slack and he lay back in the bed.

He was dying. This was when the boys were little. Aileen had heard about my father, and she'd called to tell me she was sorry. On the phone at the hospital, she asked how I was holding up and I said fine. I thought of her story about my father. Beatrice leading Dante from his dark wood. Our secret. I looked at my father asleep in the bed, a flat sheet where his left leg should've been. I sat down in a chair near the window. "Aileen, did my father really make a pass at you?" I asked.

She was quiet.

"Yes," she said finally. "But it was gentle, and I was flirting like crazy. I kept leaning my head back into his chest. I had a terrible crush on him then."

After that, Aileen and I talked about Darnell and the boys, about her recent divorce, then we hung up.

On the hospital bed, my father moved his head to the side and mumbled something about protecting my mother. His voice that time in the den coming back to me. The poet-knight, Wolfram. Our one body, one flesh and blood, doing itself much harm.

My father's eyelids fluttered—dreaming.

I drove to Mass on Good Friday, stomach knotted, hands clamped to the steering wheel. I hadn't tried communion since that time the shaking started. Father Howard saying come back when you're ready, don't rush it. I drove around the block three times trying to decide, then pulled into a Circle K and bought two peach wine coolers and downed them in the car. In front of the store, a woman in a red sundress talked on a pay phone, holding onto her little girl's shoulders. The woman's head jerked as she talked. She shouted at someone on the phone named Zachary. Then the girl wriggled free and the woman's pocketbook fell from beneath her arm, spilling change on the ground. The girl wandered over to a tire air machine and punched at the buttons. The woman looked at the girl and then saw me inside the car. I didn't look away. I wanted to say it would be all right, whatever had happened, though I knew it wasn't true. She would have to live without things. But knowing this wouldn't make it easier.

The woman hung up, gathered her change, and helped her daughter into the car.

I pulled out of the parking lot and headed toward the church. Once, I'd called Darnell's number in Austin late one night to arrange for Michael to visit, and instead of the usual answering machine, a sleepy-voiced woman answered. I stayed on for a second, listening to the line buzz, her breathing. A tiredness gathered in my shoulders, arms. Even holding the phone seemed like an effort. I hung up. Then, for some reason, the tiredness lifted and I noticed how hungry I was.

The church parking lot was full, so I turned down a neighborhood street. Two boys tossed a baseball beneath the streetlight, while a third ran feverishly between them. Hotbox, a game my sons had played. Their shouts just beyond our sliding glass door. The ball bounced into the road and I stopped the car while one of the boys grabbed it. Then, a few houses down, I saw Bill Comeaux in a suit, next to his Mazda, talking with a bald man. There had been an accident and the Mazda's headlights lit up shards of red plastic on the pavement. I pulled over, tucked the empty wine cooler bottles in the back seat and got out.

Bill had his hands in his pockets, and in the headlight glare I saw him smile at something the bald man said. Then he looked over at me, squinting. "Hey there, Kay," he said. "Thought we only saw each other at potlucks." He smiled.

"Some Good Friday, huh," I said, coming up to him. Lately, Bill had started calling our potlucks *pout in your pot sessions*. In the last year, his face had lost its haggard look. He'd trimmed up his dark hair. Even mentioned a woman he might be interested in. I'd encouraged him but now wished I hadn't.

Bill said, "You look great."

"You've been eating," I said, smiling.

On the pavement, Bill nudged some shattered remains of the accident with his foot. And for a second, he seemed to drift away. Somewhere, his wife was reaching to adjust his tie, to smooth strands of his hair. My dead son was there too.

Standing at the edge of the light, I touched Bill's hand. Held it there for a few seconds. Warm.

Tommi Ferguson

SCOTT BLACKWOOD is coordinator of the Undergraduate Writing Center at the University of Texas at Austin and has published stories in the *Boston Review, Other Voices, Gulf Coast*, and *Whetstone*. He's currently working on a novel-in-stories about the stirrings of fate and chance in the lives of Odie Dodd and his neighbors. Blackwood lives with his wife and daughter in the hills on Austin's outskirts where Tonkawa Indians once roamed. His distant relative William Blackwood founded *Blackwood's Magazine*, which first published Joseph Conrad's *Heart of Darkness* in 1899.